THE TREES TOLD ME SO

THE TREES TOLD ME SO

Purva Grover

olive turtle

NIYOGI BOOKS

Published by
NIYOGI BOOKS
Block D, Building No. 77,
Okhla Industrial Area, Phase-I,
New Delhi-110 020, INDIA
Tel: 91-11-26816301, 26818960
Email: niyogibooks@gmail.com
Website: www.niyogibooksindia.com

Editor: Manali Das
Design: Shraboni Roy
Cover image: Based on a sketch by Natanaelginting - Freepik.com

ISBN: 978-93-86906-20-5
Publication: 2018

This is a work of fiction. The names, characters and incidents portrayed in it are the work of the author's imagination. Any resemblance to actual persons, living or dead, events or localities, is entirely coincidental.

Printed at: Niyogi Offset Pvt. Ltd., New Delhi, India

To Mummy-Papa, for all the love

CONTENTS

PREFACE

Why did the trees speak to me?

Why did the characters, whose lives had been touched by the trees, decide to confide in me?

I am yet to know.

Could it be because I promised to listen closely?

I took notes of thoughts that came and vanished. I scribbled down memories that I wished we cherished. I was patient when I met up with people who ached to share. I dealt with questions that made me uncomfortable. I let the sceneries, objects and situations inspire me. I expressed joy, love, anxiety, disappointment, anger, happiness and pain.

Together, we wove these 11 tales—of faith, funeral; of dads, dreams; of growth, greed; of sins, secrets; of chai, confessions; of relationships, reflections; of lives, loves and living.

And we remembered to do so with honesty because it's only the honest words that have the power to bring about change, touch hearts and awaken minds.

I can only hope we never lose faith in these words.

These tales are now as much *yours* as they are *mine*.

THE DARKNESS OF RED

My fingers are stained with red—a rusty, dirty red. Not the kind of red that bleeds, but the one that lingers. If you were to judge me by my hands, you'd probably never talk to me. Although, I believe that you wouldn't react any differently if you were to judge me by my face. I'm a coarse man with crooked teeth, bushy eyebrows and a mole-infested forehead. Yet, despite my appearance, you'd come back to me, over and over. I have you addicted. That's what I sell—addiction.

The business of selling addiction has made many men and women rich. I came to this city with similar dreams.

I wasn't the first, and I wasn't alone. I arrived with a bunch of people wanting to challenge the high-rise buildings and grow taller than each of them, even each other. But fate had different plans for me. The city didn't enrich my life with silver buttons and gold coins.

It wasn't easy: not at the start, nor in the middle. It took me years to learn not to complain. I had many arguments with the powerful One. I complained and compared while He just sat, listening to me. I was told He sits up there, above all of us. I had to learn how to forgive Him for not being kind to me. One day, I looked up at the skies and told Him I bore no grudges against Him. That day, I learned that the view from up there is very unclear—the city skies are filled with smoke and deception.

Today, when I look at the bawdy woman who once stayed two houses away from mine in the village, I don't feel envious. Don't get me wrong. I'd still want to bed her—a woman with a full bosom and fuller hips. But her riches don't make me sad any more. She too sells addiction. When I meet her on my way from home, she laughs and says, 'I've made a fortune. I know how to trade.' Perhaps she's right; maybe she does. After all, I sell, too—to men, mostly. But not all needs are the same. My men are addicts, but their dependence on me has not resulted in me building an empire.

The woman, Swapna, has a husband too. He too seems to know the tricks of the trade. I'm not a big fan of his business; it's selling another level of addiction. I've often witnessed his clients create a ruckus at night. They arrive at odd hours and indulge in a lot of screaming and shouting. I heard that on two occasions the police had to come down to sort things out. Once, the police loaded the clients in a van and took them away. Another time, they left them out on the streets. 'They were dead,' said Swapna. 'The dogs feasted on them.' Next morning, I saw a few images in the local newspaper. The faces of the clients were covered in froth—the same kind of froth that the city soap generates when I rub it vigorously to get rid of the red on my hands. These soaps are no good.

In my city, the business of selling addiction is quite big. I once met this lanky boy of 25, who told me that he had people addicted to a life across the country waters. He drives a very, very big car. I have never seen such a big car and once, when I told him that my entire village could fit into it, he laughed at me. He thought I was joking. Perhaps he's never known a family from a village or been to a house in the village. One day, I'll invite him over. We can both go in his car. He tells me that people no longer want to live in the city, the country. They all want to go *pardes*.

One evening, I asked him to sell the addiction to me. He said, 'Chaurasia, do you want to fly and then land in a place that gleams? I will give you a ride in the clouds and transport you to the world where everything sparkles.'

I was sold. I said, 'You had sparkling teeth, once upon a time.'

He laughed, 'Yes, before I got addicted.'

I responded with a crooked smile.

Chandar has teeth with red marks, but they look nice on him; they match his very, very big red car and even his shoes. Once, I saw him with a lady in a red lehenga (later he told me it was called a skirt) too. I think he likes the colour red.

I, too, like the colour red: even when it stains the walls and covers my hands. Red has helped me build a roof over my head; it lets the sunlight filter through and keeps the rain water away. Red has helped me buy a television to watch Amitabh Bachchan. He is a superstar from my land who gives money to everyone (one day, I'll go to his house; he waves at people who gather round it) on a show that he hosts. They call it *Kaun Banega Crorepati* (*Who Wants To Be A Millionaire?*)—it is a show from *pardes*.

Red has helped me own a refrigerator for storing ice cubes. Before, I picked up ice from graveyards and stored it in an earthen pot, but it was no good. In graveyards, there's ice available always, in the form of huge slabs. Once the body is off the slab, the ice is of no use to the grave diggers. Do carry a gunny sack if you want it.

Everyone calls me Chaurasia, but that's not my first or last name. It's a name the city gave me, and you can never say no to what the city gives you.

Forty-three years ago, when I took a bus to the city, I told the bus conductor, 'I know how to roll paan.' He said, 'Oh! Chaurasia babu.' The people who sat and stood around me seemed to recognise me. It made me very happy. At my destination, I was to meet my childhood friend from the village (he had left five years ago). But I couldn't find him. In cities, people often get lost. It's not like in the villages, where you wake up and take bath together at a tube well. If we were still at the village, I would recognise him taking a bath—naked and wrinkled. I miss him.

Nobody ever taught me how to roll betel leaves. The creeper consumed the rod on which the hay roof stood. My grandfather watered the heart-shaped leaves every now and then. When he wasn't doing that, he was rolling the leaves. I don't know if anyone taught him how to fold a leaf either, he just knew it. He'd lift the bottom right corner of the leaf to cover the centre, and then do the same with the left corner and place it on top of the previous fold. He'd twist it, tuck it and eat it. It really was that simple. 'Don't press it too hard,' he used to tell anyone who cared to listen. I did.

I think every man and woman in my family knew how to transform the heart into a triangle—just like we all knew how to smoke a pipe. I learnt that chewing paan was not an expensive pastime. On the few days when there was nothing for us to eat, my mother would hand over paan to us. We'd each take a leaf, soaked in the water tumbler, and use a twig to coat it with *chuna*, followed by *kattha* and occasionally, sweet powder, which is a concoction of sugar, rose leaves, menthol and red food colour. After rubbing on a little *heera panna*, we'd fold and eat it. We never slept on an empty stomach.

We weren't the poorest in the village, but when I turned 17, I realised that a paan tasted better when consumed after a meal—a meal comprising roti, dal and onion. I told this to my mother. The same evening, she tied up a bundle for me—two torn shirts and a pyjama. She also gave me ₹2. I boarded a bus to the city.

It was a hot summer day. I made an attempt to stare at the sun; it left my eyes teary. My skin burnt too. I spent the entire hot day looking for my friend. I called him from a public phone booth and went to the address he'd described. By the time the sun set, I was tired. I was also sure that he would find me, friends always find a way.

I walked into a gurudwara to eat a meal and drink water; the *langar* lulled the cramps in my stomach. I wish they'd let me sleep there too because even though the sun was resting, it was still very hot. A tree befriended me that night; its branches kept me cool. I tried to sleep under it, but there were numerous motor vehicles that ran on the nearby road. They kept honking and flashing their lights into my face. I tossed and turned, and must have fallen asleep facing the trunk of the tree.

When I woke up, the vehicles were still honking, but the lights were now off. I wiped the beads of sweat from my face with my shirt and walked up to the address my friend had given me. He still wasn't there.

I began to think maybe he'd been run over by a motor in his sleep, under a tree. It wasn't safe to *simply* lie under the tree. I needed a roof. That night, I made myself a roof. I hung the shirt on one of the branches and laid down the cloth that had wrapped the bundle on the ground. At night, I sat in my home and watched the motors, and even tried to count them. I thought to myself, 'This city has more motors than birds.' I chewed on three paans that day. Chewing paan doesn't make you feel hungry. I was to learn that chewing gum also had the same effect. I felt safe and fell asleep early; lethargy and boredom induce sleep. For the next few days, I followed the same routine. My friend was still missing, my money was intact, and I'd almost finished my betel leaves and condiments.

In a city, few things last; most diminish gradually.

I stared at my two bundles of betel leaves and wondered if I could arrange for money to return home. The *langar* was simple and tasty, but I had to return home. Sitting under *my* tree, I scribbled 'Chaurasia' in the mud (I had attended school for a couple of years and knew how to write the alphabets and count the days, money and betel leaves) when a motor blew a deafening horn in my ears. 'Chaurasia, *do paan dena*,' said a head popping out of a half-open window.

In cities, people shamelessly take from the poor and ask favours of strangers. Uncertain how to react, I laid flat two wet leaves and coated them with *chuna, kattha* and *heera panna.* I put two *suparis*, each in the centre, folded it and handed it over to the popping head, worrying I'd have nothing to eat for lunch. The popping head threw a coin (denomination of 50 paisa) towards me, and drove on. I was startled. In my village, no one had ever given me money for rolling paan. I realised the city was indeed a strange place.

That same evening, the motor returned again. I rolled up two more paans. At night, when I went to the gurudwara to eat, I laid a coin at the feet of the powerful One.

Next morning, I rolled up four leaves and waited for the man in the motor. He was pleased to see me prepared.

A fortnight later, a handful of men in motors had consumed the last two bundles. I began to identify them by the numbers on their motor plates. With nothing more to sell, I boarded a bus to my village. When my mother saw me at the door, she cried and hugged me. My father was disheartened to see me return, and said the men in the village would laugh at me. But when I took out a five-rupee note from my pocket and put it in his hand, he rolled up his moustache and walked out of the door. My grandfather was unhappy with me. He told my grandmother that

I was disgracing the family name by selling paan; you never sell paan, you offer it as a gesture. I didn't tell him that I had a new name, too. I feared he would never speak to me again. I returned to the city the next morning with a bigger bundle of leaves and a cardboard box carrying all the condiments.

Under my tree, I put up a new roof, made with blue plastic bags. I used the wood from the branches to define a boundary and arranged a dozen boxes of condiments by it. On the backside of the cardboard box, I wrote 'Chaurasia Paan' with *kattha.* Now each time a motor stopped, I'd hand over a neatly rolled paan, and say, '*Aap ke liye,* Chaurasia paan.' The men now gave me the coin in my hand instead of throwing it towards me. A few even smiled at me. The city was turning warmer towards me and the weather colder. I was rolling 33 paans a day and making one trip, every three months, to my village. My mother cried on every visit; even when I handed over a bright red dupatta to her, she cried. My father's moustache was always rolled upwards. He'd sit on a charpoy under the tree where my grandfather used to sit, smoking his pipe and chewing paan.

My grandfather died an unhappy man. He never approved of my city doings, but he ended his days in a warm blanket I'd brought him from the city. On his death bed, I asked him if he knew what the word 'Chaurasia' meant. It made him very angry. He spat his paan residue vehemently on the floor and told me only rascals make a city home by selling paans, not only to men, but women also. I never told him of the board that now hung on my tree branch; I even put a torch there for clients who craved paan at night. His last few words gave me an idea. Back in the city, I began to offer paan to the women who sat in the motors with the men. They smiled at me, but then spat the paan all over my boundary wall, board and tree. I was disappointed.

A few months later, when, on my visit home, my mother arranged my marriage to a girl, I rolled a paan for her on our wedding night. She didn't spit it out on my sparkling white kurta, but told me that next time I should make it sweeter. I grinned, showing her my red teeth. The next day, when we left for the city, I carried with me boxes of *kesari supari*, sweet powder—a mixture of sugar, perfumed water and menthol, *shahad, khajoor, sookha nariyal* and *gulkand.*

I found wisdom in the words 'lady luck'. I was now selling *saada* and meetha addiction to men and women, respectively. We stayed in a tin-roofed shed, close to the tree. At the wedding, when her mother gifted a *choolah* to her, I stopped eating the *langar.*

The city had become noisier and fuller over time. The handful of birds still chirped, and the owners of the motors, scooters, cycles and rickshaws gave me good business. They told me how there was magic in my hands and they were addicted to Chaurasia paan. I knew most of my customers by either of three names now: first, last or humorous. They'd stand for minutes and hours around my shop, and talk endlessly about their lives.

I was a happy man. My wife had given me a boy. At night, I'd tell my boy that the city was our home. In the mornings, I'd dream of a *pucca ghar.*

A few of my customers said that coming to my shop was better than reading a newspaper; anything that happened in the city was discussed here. I didn't know if that was true. And whilst they all spoke of the same thing, they never agreed with each other. A few said building flyovers was a good development; it would help the city reach the moon. A handful told me how construction was making them rich; they told me not to mention this to anyone else. A soft-spoken woman warned me to look for another spot because the government would be chopping down the trees to make the motors fly on raised ground. I couldn't sleep that night.

The next morning, she came back to the shop. This time she told me that the flyover completed last month had come cracking down on the people and the motors. She said, 'Chaurasia bhai, you can stop worrying for some time. They won't build another flyover anytime soon.' I found out the flyover had killed 12 men, three women and five children, and injured another 50. I told my wife that chopping down trees was a horrible thing to do. Without the shade of a tree, I would not have survived.

I had now been in the city for 13 summers and winters and borne two boys; both learnt to roll paans. I named them Ram Lal Chaurasia (Ram being the seventh *avatar* of the Hindu God Vishnu and a king of Ayodhya and 'lal' meaning red) and Kamal Lal ('kamal' meaning lotus) Chaurasia. In the afternoons, when they returned from school, I would send them to pick up supplies for the paans from a wholesale city shop near the railway station. I'd long ago stopped bringing supplies from the village. In the evenings, I'd let them sit with me and even assist me at my Chaurasia Paan House. At nights, I would send them to sleep with their mother.

A few of my customers said coming to my shop inspired them to compose poetry. 'There's nothing better than the combination of a juicy paan and a lit cigarette.' They said it was here they watched life pass by. They'd talk loudly, dress shabbily and curse incessantly. Many times, they'd walk off without paying for the paan and ask me to write down the amount in my book. My elder son maintained this book and he often told me that one day these poets and writers would leave me with nothing. A few of them even showed me their pictures in the newspaper. I asked a poet to bring over a cinema actress. They were both starring in the same film. And one night, he brought her for a meetha paan. She was delighted with my sweet preparation. To please her, I had added *saunf* to it. The next day, her picture at my paan shop appeared in the paper. My face wasn't visible; the yellow bulb hanging in the shop had blocked it. The next day, I bought a white tube light.

After that day, cinema people began to visit me frequently. I asked my elder son to sit with me at the shop every day. I also stopped keeping accounts of the money due to me from poets and writers. I'd listen attentively to them. They spoke of the joys of comparing the beauty of a beloved to the moon, and the miseries of attaining fame, yet returning to an empty palace.

I didn't understand their complex words, but I continued to be an appreciative admirer. One writer told me that Lord Buddha attained enlightenment under a tree. It made me feel important. The city makes everyone feel important. We all need each other to survive. If the poor were well fed, then how would the rich get a chance to flaunt their wealth? They feed us, the poor, to please their stars, a man at the gurudwara once told me.

A few of my customers confessed that it was only at my shop, where no one would watch them, that they could find lovers. My shop was always brimming with conversations. I found it hard to believe that no one was watching them here. But then I'd discovered how easy it was to get lost in a crowd. Three decades, and I still hadn't found my friend. These men and women often came late at night; sometimes the men drove, occasionally the women, rarely the driver. They looked happy and their eyes shone with love; they shone even when they arrived with different men and women, every other week. I couldn't comprehend that kind of love. The only woman I had loved was my wife. And the only woman I had lusted after was Swapna. When I told my wife that these men and women had both lovers and spouses, she closed her eyes in disbelief and said a prayer. She asked me what would happen if they were to find out about each other. I smiled. The city keeps everyone's secrets. No one knows my first and last name. That night, I dreamt of Swapna. I felt lucky. I had a life, I had a dream. I had become less greedy, more content. I shared this with Swapna—her laughter was bitter and seductive.

A few of my customers spoke only in numbers. They were big businessmen. They all knew Swapna too. Their phones always kept ringing. They carried the public phone booths in the pockets of their shirts, I told my wife. This time too, she rubbed her eyes in disbelief and said a prayer. A few weeks later, her prayer was answered. I bought her a phone booth she could tie in at the end of her saree. These men carried bundles of notes and often paid me without even counting either the notes or the paans. I attempted to bring their notice to it, but they wouldn't listen; they were too busy talking numbers. They asked me who my target customer was. Not knowing what to say, I replied, 'You!' I simply wanted to please them. They seemed pleased. They taught me that in every business there were competitors and cheaters. The same night, I asked my son to make me a new board for my shop; this time in English. It read 'Chaurasia Paan Bhandar: We have no branches'. A few weeks later, a fat man who carried two phones asked me to prefix 'Chaurasia Paan Bhandar' with the word 'original'. I did so. By now, although there were five Chaurasia Paan Bhandar shops in the neighbourhood, mine was the only 'original'.

The city makes space for everyone. Under each tree, there was space for one seller and many addicts. I felt that as long as there were trees in the city, there would be space for each village man to lay down a piece of cloth and sleep under the smoky sky.

There were also customers I turned down. I used to scare pregnant women by showing them the gory images that the government had started printing on cigarette packs. If I were to sell cigarettes to them, I feared my grandfather's ghost would haunt me. I was now selling paans, cigarettes and gum. I also learned a lot from my customers. A man in his thirties, who worked in a bank, bought me a pair of gloves to wear while prepping the paan. A few weeks after I'd worn the plastic on my hands, he persuaded me to sign a few papers and said he could now get me money to build a shop with bricks and cement. A young girl who always wore cheerful-coloured kurtas gifted me a certificate in a glass box. She said from now on I could tell everyone that my paans were hygienic and the best in the city. Most people were kind to me.

One night, when I was closing the shutters of my shop to go home, I saw a motor run over the people sleeping on the street. This time, I was the one closing my eyes and saying a prayer. The next morning, I appeared on television. I was asked if I could narrate what I'd seen the previous night. My mother had always told me not to meddle in other people's affairs. I told the TV people that I hadn't seen anything. I wish my grandfather had been alive to watch me on TV. A few days later, the circus continued on the street, with many people inspecting the site. Some sat for hours without food and water; some just stood and talked. The circus helped me pay for my sons' higher education.

When someone in a city dies, no one notices. Every dead body is replaced by a living one.

I was content with my action. If I'd taken part in the circus, I would have lost my shop, my home, my family. I was no longer greedy, but I was needy.

Meanwhile, a few of my customers told me I had become modern. The paans were now wrapped in a transparent sheet and carried in a paper napkin.

I had made the city of addicts my home.

Sitting under the tree now, I sometimes wonder whether I should return to my village to chew paan and smoke a pipe under the tree; just like my grandfather and father.

But I don't know if I can ever return. I also don't know how long I'll live.

I ask myself: has selling addiction made me rich?

My wife wears gold *bali*s. I drive a two-wheeler.

I ask myself: am I different from my cousins in the village?

When they attended the wedding of my sons, they told me I was now a *babu,* a gentleman. And having served them alcohol from a tall glass bottle, they called me an *angrez,* a foreigner.

I ask myself: did the city help me fulfill my dreams?

My sons are the only educated men from the village.

I ask myself: can I roll what I've earned in the city into a bundle, and board a bus back to the village?

I realise that whilst I can still gather up my belongings, I wouldn't be able to carry the weight of the city with me. The secrets of the rich, the deceptions of the beloved, the greed of the successful, the pain of the poets, the dreams of the young, the miseries of the old, the energy of the poor, the joys of alcohol, the emptiness of the powerful, the sound of the bangles, the rings of the phones, the peace of the hermit, and the darkness of the red.

I look up at the tree with many branches and fewer leaves. I look at my shop with no 'branches' and myself with fewer teeth. And then I look at my hands, covered in red. What will I tell my village men? What will I show them I've gained? Can you read the lines of a hand under a cloud of red? Will they forgive me for selling paans?

I don't have answers to these questions, so I decide to stay back.

I don't fret. I don't look back. Now, I have just two hopes: one, to find my friend. If he's wealthy, I'll forgive him for forgetting me; the city does that to some of us. If he's poor, I'll ask my wife to cook a meal for him on the *choolah.*

Two, to meet and thank the rascal called Chaurasia.

Before I roll my last paan, will the city fulfill my wishes?

I don't know. The city has a mind of its own.

***

I spent my life under a once-flowering jamun tree.

I wonder whether I should tell you the name by which my parents and grandparents called me. I wonder whether I should tell you the name of the city where this tree was once planted.

But then I stop myself; in a city, many are nameless.

*****

A SUMMER RITUAL

I am sitting on a couch in the verandah; the couch is not in its usual spot in the living room. In fact, nothing is, and I want to whine about it. I want everyone to stand up, wipe those tears and put things in order. 'Who moved the potted plants from the verandah?' I think to myself, getting annoyed, 'and where's the hose pipe?'

From the outside, I can see a large serving tray, full of tea cups, on the centre table in the living room, 'Granny would have never served tea in those cups.' This mess is making me upset and angry. I look around at the sea of people and tears. It doesn't seem like anyone is going to get up, not for a while at least. It's a hot day, a hot July afternoon, and they're going to sit here hoping that the very hot tea will bring them comfort.

'Where are the potted plants?' I say out aloud, knowing no one is listening.

Two wheeled stretchers are occupying the spot of the pots. 'Can someone remove them?' I hear my voice, going unnoticed again. I walk out of the gates muttering, 'Why are the stretchers still there? They have no use, not any more.'

This was 'our' last summer together: Granny's, Grandpa's and mine; and this is not how it should have gone. Granny was 76 and Grandpa was 80, I, 22. When the old die, they die of heart strokes, not in accidents. I didn't want to hear anything of the road accident. I wanted to blame someone for the mess and since, this someone had absconded from the site, I decided there was nothing I wanted to do with it. The chapter was over. They had decided to go away, together, and I will have to live with it. No questions asked, no answers sought.

I was at their home, just a few weeks before and they'd waved me off, teary eyed. I study at the university and my summer break was just a week, so I had spent only a day with them before heading back to my classes. I sat in the taxi with a heavy heart and a choked throat. 'See you next year, Granny,' I'd said. Over the years, I had noticed my grandfather was finding it harder to hide his tears, Granny was always okay with crying.

'So, Granny was right,' I thought to myself on the way back to the university, after attending their funeral. 'The tree was older than both of them.' My grandparents' home had a mango tree with cheerful yellow flowers. When I was three, Granny told me the tree was 200 years old. 'The tree can't be older than Grandpa,' I told her. I thought Grandpa was 150.

The tree occupied the centre of their home. It was encircled by two bedrooms, one living room, a kitchen and two bathrooms. And regardless of the room you'd just left, you'd find yourself facing the tree. Sheltering the verandah at a height of more than 20 feet, it looked over the house and each one of us. The verandah had a small metal tap with a hose pipe permanently attached to it. Grandpa would use it to water the tree, and on hot summer days when he washed its dark-green leaves, he'd let us, grandchildren, stand underneath and get drenched. It was my favourite summer game.

Summer was special; the time we'd all gather at their home. And there was always space for everyone: two aunts, two uncles, Mum, Dad and six grandchildren. I spent 18 'full' summers with Granny, Grandpa and the mango tree. And while everything around us changed, we stuck to this one routine.

It was a simple routine; a ritual that involved booking train (later, flight) tickets, packing bags and spending a few weeks in their home. None of us ever spoke of the worth of its existence or the consequences if it were to be discontinued. There was no need to discuss the 'usual'.

However, it was the one ritual that summed up the meaning of the words 'togetherness', 'family' and 'patience' for me. A bunch of individuals in different age groups and with different temperaments spending a few moments under one roof, acknowledging and overlooking each other's limitations and applauding the goodness. It was in those summer months, I learnt that as a family, we were meant to forgive and forget, and blossom together—irrespective of our egos, ambitions, differences, challenges, dreams and insecurities. The fact that there could ever be a change in this evenness never occurred to me, until that last summer.

Each May, I'd receive a letter from Granny saying she was waiting for us to visit in June and July, when the schools were closed. As we arrive, she'd be standing with Grandpa at the gates to welcome us. When our train was delayed, she'd still wait for our taxi, sometimes for hours. As soon as the taxi took the final right turn, I'd look out of the window and spot her standing in the sun. She'd wave at me and I'd wave back, jumping with happiness and excitement. Once I'd stepped down from the taxi, she'd envelop me in a warm hug. She never let that change. And at the end of our two-month visit, when we'd packed our things into the taxi, she'd hug us again, only this time she'd cry. As I held back my own tears, I'd reassure her, 'See you next year, Granny.' A year was a long time, we both knew that. As she and Grandpa stood at the gate, they'd wave at us till the taxi took a left turn and slowly, was out of sight.

When I look back over the many summers we spent together, I'm reminded of the sequence of changes in Granny's home. When my maternal uncle and aunt (both younger than my mum) married and had kids, Grandpa announced it was time to create more space. The walls of the two bedrooms were brought down. The plain ceramic tiles in the house gave way to shiny-white marble flooring. Since Granny was in charge of the kitchen, she demanded a modern cooking range to prepare meals for her grandkids, so the old stove went too. There were more rooms, but they were smaller. The living room held two couches and four chairs, modern and plush. The dining area was now bigger, with 12 chairs. The home was prettier, brighter and more comfortable than it had ever been.

Granny and Grandpa continued to welcome us and the changes we suggested or demanded with open hearts and arms. I often wondered if it hurt them to replace older items, but when I asked Grandpa about it one day, he just smiled and kissed my forehead. However, I found the answer to my question when I was 12 and Granny opened the special cupboard with all the stuff for the grandchildren. It was filled with things we liked and needed: caramel cookies, chocolate bars, potato wafers, pencil colours, story books, kitchen sets, baby lotions, soft towels, pack of balloons, buntings and half-finished drawings from previous years. Over the years, she added internet cards, mobile chargers, diet-free cola cans, flyers for DVD rentals, pizza and pasta menu cards, and coffee sachets and mugs. I told Mum that the exception to 'no place like home' was the grandparents' place, where everything was smothered with love and care.

There was never a fixed time that we kids had to be out of bed at Granny and Grandpa's, but we'd always be up early. A stereo system would be playing in the verandah and they'd both be preparing for the day, listening to a radio station airing old Hindi songs and boring advertisements for oils and batteries. 'Oh, did we wake you up?' was their way of saying, 'Go back to bed if you like.'

Rubbing my eyes, I'd sit under the spreading tree on a red and brown *chatai*. I'd watch Granny arrange thin potato slices on a bedsheet so they'd dry in the sunlight filtering through the branches. At night, she'd roll up the sheet and keep it in the kitchen. A fortnight later, she'd fry these slices and bring them to us on a plate to eat. I still remember crunching and licking the masala off these homemade wafers, and we always had a packet for the journey home.

I liked sitting next to Granny, absorbing the sounds of the morning: a bird cuckooing, a vegetable vendor calling, a milkman honking and a tea pot brewing. Granny would be wearing the salwar-kameez she'd slept in. The breeze wasn't warm at that hour and the birds would chirp softly from the tree or the sheet of potato slices, until the grandchildren shooed them away. We'd sing the poems and rhymes we'd learnt at school to Granny as she made breakfast. 'So, what class are you in now?' she'd ask from the kitchen window. And no matter which grade we'd made, she'd tell Grandpa, 'Oh, what big girls and boys they are now,' as he nodded in appreciation.

One summer, I decided to play a prank, telling her I'd changed schools, to see if she remembered the name of the one I was at. 'Oh, so you'll miss your friend Swati,' she said, peeping out from the kitchen window. I realised that not only was she a patient listener, but also an attentive one. Granny and Grandpa never forgot anything, from the food we liked to the friends we made. As we grew up, we told them about our school annual days, favourite teachers, university scholarships and hostel mates. No matter what we shared, they took it on board. They'd memorise the names of the courses we studied and the colleges we attended, sharing these details with the neighbours, exuding pride.

As we spoke non-stop, Grandpa would fetch breakfast for us and leave to dress for work. Granny would make stuffed paranthas and mango milkshake for us—our special breakfast for all the days that we were there. Granny herself taught at a university. One day, I saw her checking bundles of exam papers. When I asked her if she was busy, she immediately swept the papers aside and said she was eager to learn how to write one to 10 from me. 'It'll help me when I allot the marks,' she said. The fact that when we were there, she would take an off from her regular duties at the university was another given.

The mornings would give way to noon sooner than we'd realise. And each time I try to recall what we did until Grandpa returned from work, I add to a list of happy memories. We played our favourite games, Ludo and Snakes & Ladders, most of which ended with disputes that Granny would have to resolve. She'd distract us with colouring books and drawing pads. Soon we'd be busy making flowers, playgrounds, rainbows, stars, classrooms and mountains. Granny would then ask us to write down our names on small pieces of paper to decide the order in which we'd shower. The sun would be harsh and we'd be sweating, but we put off showering for fear of missing out on something. Somewhere amid all this noise and fun, a bowl with hot oil would appear to be rubbed on our scalps and hair. And just like that many afternoons would vanish.

As mobile phones became our friends, Granny shared nuggets from the fights we had as kids and showed us greetings cards we'd made for them; all kept safe in their hearts and cupboards. I now watched my younger cousins sitting under the tree, finishing their holiday homework. A few of us were now sitting for exams and attending colleges, so it was tougher to gather at their home for longer durations. Yet, they never complained when the visits shortened; they said they were just happy to see us, all of us, the family they'd nurtured.

Meanwhile, Grandpa retired from his position as principal of the college, and began riding his old bicycle to a library where he worked towards preserving the books that were torn and forgotten. He always parked the cycle under the tree when he arrived home at lunch time. His students at the college owned scooters, motorbikes and cars, but he said he liked commuting on his old companion. He brought the car out from the garage when he took us out for an evening of chilled flavoured milk. We'd drive to the shop, he'd hand us ₹1 or ₹2, and we were free to use it as we liked. We had many bottles and flavours of milk in those summer months.

We'd know he was home if his bicycle was resting its weight on the tree bark. We'd also know that soon it'd be time to climb the tree. He'd bring me books to read and I'd sit in the shade of the tree, flipping through them excitedly while he rested in his bedroom. I could see him through the bedroom window, and waited till he was fast asleep before calling out to my elder sibling and cousins to climb the tree. This was how we filled our afternoons after Granny went to take a nap, having fed us happy meals, and the house was quiet. We'd drag the ladder from the garage and begin to ascend. The first to reach the lowest branch would be asked to shake it vigorously to make the mangoes fall, till either there were enough on the ground for all of us or Granny would wake up and start making tea for her and Grandpa.

When she found us, we'd tell her a strong wind had blown many mangoes down. She'd always pretend to be surprised, 'I'm glad you were asleep inside so the mangoes didn't fall on your tiny heads. Be careful next time there's a storm.' She'd also ignore the ladder lying on the ground. She'd ask us to help her collect the mangoes, putting them in a giant blue bucket filled with cold water.

Half an hour later, dressed in home clothes, we'd sit around the container full of juicy fruits. Granny would sit on a small pew, teaching us how to eat them. 'You should always enjoy a mango, not just eat it,' she'd say. Next to her would be a big brass vessel to hold the mangoes that were not good enough to be eaten by us. She'd share out the ones that were yellow in colour with spots of red, and keep aside the very red, yellow and green, and yellowish-orange ones. When we each had a mango in our little hands, she'd demonstrate how best to engage with it. 'Squeeze firmly. Now, knead the mango and feel its scintillating flesh and juice.' We'd puncture and rupture the peel, hoping to do better with the next one. Then we'd bring the mango to our mouths and bite a small hole in the top, from which it was possible to suck the juice. 'Slurp firmly,' she'd say. When the juice was over, we'd peel the skin and scrape its soft underside for our next pleasurable treat. Lastly, we'd pull all the juice and flesh from the mango seed. After what seemed like several hours of mango eating, our stomachs would be full, hands sticky and faces messy. Tufts of mango would be stuck in our teeth and our clothes would be marked by the juice. 'It is shower time,' Granny would announce as she opened the verandah tap. We'd hose each other down and jump in the puddles while she returned to the kitchen with her vessel. Exhausted with eating, jumping and bathing, we'd fall asleep for a few hours and the home would be quiet again.

On waking up, we'd find Grandpa standing on the ladder, tying a rope on the branch. 'A home with grandchildren isn't complete without a swing,' he'd say. Once when I asked him why he went through the pain of tying and untying the swing each year, he told me he wanted to select the best branch. Weeks before we arrived, he'd study the branches from trunk to tip. The ones showing signs of disease, splitting or narrow connections to the main trunk were instantly dismissed. Once he'd found a healthy branch which was large enough to hold the swing, at least a couple of inches away from the trunk, he'd climb up the ladder. Using a thick rope, he'd suspend a wooden plank from the branch for us to swing on. The wooden plank was later replaced with a plastic seat, followed by a readymade swing that came with hooks and didn't require any knots. 'In my grandparents' home, we had a swing made out of an old tyre,' Granny told me once.

Night would soon fall, and the sun and the playing would have sapped all the energy we had. Unwilling to retire to our rooms, we'd coax Granny to tell us a story. 'Just one story and we promise to eat dinner and sleep,' we'd say in unison. Granny too would be tired at the end of the day, but she'd never refuse.

Once again, we would sit under the tree, this time on a *manjaa*, her in the middle, us huddled around. She always had many stories to tell, and never read from a book. We'd travel to her parents' home in the village, to the moon, to the house of friendly bears, but mostly, to the land of princes and princesses with the same names as ours. And when we rubbed our eyes, she'd feed us dinner and we'd fall asleep in her lap, under the tree.

Next morning, we'd wake up excited and do the same things, all over again, never tiring of them. Granny would have used the mangoes from the brass vessel and created yellow goodness from them: juices, pickles, jams and squashes. Mango ice cream topped with mango cubes was my favourite, and we'd eat it every day.

I am 25, now. The eldest of us, grandchildren, is married and the youngest is the only one in school now. We're all grown-ups. It's been three years since I visited my grandparents' home, which now has more rooms and fancier lights. My maternal uncle and his family live there now. They invite all of us to visit them, and each summer, I decline. The mango tree was axed and the verandah was covered to make space. And I know that it was the right thing to do, but I don't know how to return.

There's nothing left for me to go back to.

I know I'm too old to swing, but I imagine swinging on the wooden plank. I look back and see Grandpa standing behind and pushing gently. 'Hold the rope,' he says. And I go higher in the sky.

I can taste the crunchy potato wafers and see myself asking Granny for more, each day. 'I can never get enough of your special preparations,' I say. I scour through the treasure in Granny's cupboard. I wait for Grandpa to turn on the tap and drench me. I know they're just memories. I know there'll be no more letters and no more hugs at the gate. But I also know that living with memories is easier; it brings me peace.

I am reminded of the hot tea cups on that tray, that July afternoon; identifying comforting elements seems tricky now.

I talk to my cousins, aunts and uncles, every now and then, but we don't meet up as often, everyone *is* busy. 'Did we meet only because Granny and Grandpa wished for us to?' Our schedules are hectic. We all need to blame someone for this discontinuity in the summer routine, so we blame time and distance. No questions asked, no answers sought.

Sometimes, I wish there was a big dispute between all of us to explain the mess. Why don't we meet now? Or were there always differences between us that needed attention? Perhaps, Granny and Grandpa were the only ones who knew how to resolve them. I try to recall the expressions that we wore; were we in it only because we feared the old die of heart strokes?

I decide I don't want to dwell into it; whimpering and going over each word, argument and hug, wondering if it were ever genuine, wondering why we never discussed the consequences of the discontinuity in the summer routine. But, on slower days, I do wonder. I wonder if summer months would have still been the same if my grandparents were alive.

And I hear my voice going unnoticed again, 'Granny and Grandpa taught us well, it's us who took the lessons poorly. Somewhere in between those summer months, we began to forget what families were meant to be.'

We all need rituals, I know that, yet I don't know how to return. But I know I was fortunate to have spent my summers in my grandparents' home and its mango tree, with all the promises, routines and cherishing.

I know the couch did find its place back in the living room, just like I found the courage to leave its comfort and attend the funeral of my grandparents—to wave goodbye, even though this time there was no waving back.

I also know that by now the couch because of overuse must be sagging, demanding a quick, easy fix. I think of the sturdy hardwood back frame, wondering if it *was* one that *could* rot. But yes, the upholstery would have come apart and the coil springs make a squeaky sound. I think of ways to fix it—a fibre board on the back, a bunch of shiny screws, a fresh lookalike fabric or a new foam padding. Or does it need to be covered in a web of cloth tape, all across—back, front and bottom? I shudder at the thought of not being able to bring it back to life, at the idea of purchasing a new one to replace the old.

***

Once, I sat under the mango tree. I read a book so dear, with a page still marked—the story isn't over, not yet. The calendar tells me it's time to return, but I fear it's too soon. The humble road leads me to their home. The hinges on the gate still make a creaking sound. I close my eyes to visit the place that was once my grandparents' home. It's cold now. The open verandah is long gone; nothing to let the rays in. No *manjaa* standing under the tree, no cuddles. I can't smell the mangoes, and there's no one to taste their sweetness. I sense the quietness in the air. Nobody's following the summer rituals. The cycle is parked in the garage, the old companion, unmet. Every now and then,

I close my eyes to visit the place that was once my grandparents' home. I look for them, I look for my tree, I look for my family and it seems as if the taxi has halted at the wrong address.

*****

A GLASS FOR ₹1

A handful of corroded stones rub against the smooth lumps of mud. A rusty frond shivers in the murkiness. A tiny ant limps to find its way out of the brown waters. Just then, I throw in a pebble in the dirty puddle, and sit and watch the ripples disturb the harmony. The pebble hits the stones making a weak sound, the frond sinks and soars, and the ant fights to keep balance. A few seconds later, when calm returns to the puddle, I throw in another pebble. In the last five days, I have played this game more than a few hundred times. At other times, I have exposed my hands to the dirty waters to watch my fingers shrivel up and later, sat down to make a comparison between my wrinkled hands and stale prunes. And in between these routine activities, I've also tried to prove useful to Gopal.

'It'll be five days today,' I shouted out to Gopal. I don't think he heard me. He was always busy, and busier on hot days like these. He wiped away the drops of the salty, colourless sweat on his forehead, pressed the lever and filled three more glasses of water, and handed them over to his customers. It was a really hot day.

Gopal owned a water trolley. It was painted in dull silver; the paint chipped at many places. The untidy, faded script on the front of the trolley read 'मशीन का ठंडा पानी' (Refrigerated Cold Water). I don't think he knew how to read and write, but he insisted on telling each of his customers that his trolley was licensed, pointing to 'LICENCED' written in bold blue, next to 'एक रु ग्लास' (A glass for ₹1). No one in the city would give you anything in return for ₹1, except this particular man and his fellow brothers.

When he didn't hear me the third time, I got impatient. 'Do you even know that five days make a full working week?' It annoyed him: the repetitive trick worked. He looked up at me, then returned to the activity of filling and cleaning glasses. I had him 'listening' now.

In the past week, he'd become my friend. We were on a first name basis. Actually, he hadn't asked me my last name and I hadn't asked his. I confess, under normal circumstances, I wouldn't even tell you that I'd found a friend in Gopal, let alone mention that I was keeping busy by assisting him in his work. I was spending my days under a lifeless coconut tree. But these weren't normal circumstances. So, I wasn't ashamed of this friendship, of being seen around him. I needed him more than he needed me. He was always surrounded by people. Perhaps, he didn't need me at all. He heard me talk continually, nodding and replying only when I pushed him with remarks that resulted in fine lines on his forehead. He smiled occasionally, never lost his temper and shared scarcely.

We were roommates, sharing a five-by-four-feet spot under a tree that faced a seven-feet-tall iron gate. It was the private spot of the public space that he owned. He set up his trolley here, outside the city hospital, a week ago, and that's the day I met him for the first time. He let me spend my days there, next to him. At nights, I felt uncomfortable, and while Gopal slept peacefully on his spot behind the trolley, I'd pace up and down until my legs, or head, or both began to hurt. Then I would settle down on the large rock facing his feet. He never complained of my pacing up and down disturbing his sleep.

I noticed his feet were cracked; there were peels of his skin on the rock and the ground, in the air, too. It disgusted me. I detested lying next to such filth, yet each night, I fell asleep there. I lacked the courage to sleep in my own bed, in my air-conditioned room.

Outside, under the skies, it wasn't just hot, but humid too; that muggy time of year when the monsoon is uncertain on whose side it wants to be—pure, joyous abundance or raw, burning havoc. The ground was always wet, the rock damp. One day, when I stood up from sitting on the rock, Gopal told me the dampness had left an ugly spot on the back of my trousers. The next day, clouds poured right on the glass of my spectacles, leaving me bungled.

Water was playing ugly games with me. The glasses of water were extinguishing my thirst, yet leaving me parched. I was confiding in a water seller and resting on a damp rock, yet the water was nothing else but a curse in my eyes. I looked up at the wilting tree, knowing it would agree. Over-watering had snatched it of everything too; it had lost a majority of its firm green leaves, just a few flaccid brown ones remained. Underneath, the soil bore hints of pale green, slowly giving way to algae. Its stunted and rotting roots suggested it would soon be dead, leaving us homeless. I might be around to see that, I thought to myself.

I was beginning to seek wisdom from the many glasses that Gopal sold each day, for just ₹1 each. Icy plain water for the simple, brackish nimbu paani for the terse, piquant jal jeera for the adventurous, sugary nimbu paani for the sweet, mineral water bottles for the status conscious, and disposable glasses for the environmentally unconscious and hygiene conscious. Each glass had a story—sprinkled with *pudina, jeera, cheeni, namak, mitti, gulab* and *pasina.* I stood there, absorbing each chapter, each life. Water that could nourish could also kill; it was hard to accept this harsh fact. The cold glass of water calmed my bitter heart and tongue, but only for a short while. As for Gopal, he went on with his work unperturbed; he never mentioned how little business I gave him—just ₹3 a day. He never asked me any questions; he just let me be. He became a part of my story. Little did I know that this was *our* story.

I knew he'd listen to mine, so I began to babble again. 'It was 10 years ago that a glass of water changed my life—I'd found my *forever.* She played volleyball—sturdy hands, delicate waist and short hair. She was sweating profusely, talking excitedly. She'd won an inter-college match. She was happy, laughing—not a sweet, delicate laugh, but a loud and unpolished cackle. She gulped down a large glass of water, then another, and another. She sat on her two-wheeler and drove inside the gates of the women's hostel, forgetting to pay. I paid for the three glasses of water she had. She noticed me, but didn't acknowledge it, just like you don't notice me, Gopal. I was a lanky boy. No one paid attention to me. She was bold and beautiful. On the field, she competed with both men and women. She dressed like a boy, as if she was one of us. I remember wondering how she'd look in a woman's outfit. It's a decade-old tale, from a time when one of your brothers, another water seller, played anchor for me. Do you still want to hear it, Gopal?' I was convinced he would reply now.

Gopal put a handful of glasses in an old, huge stainless steel tub and began to wash them. He used a dark-pink liquid soap. He had clean hands, unlike his feet.

I poured myself a fill from the trolley. It was simple; just push a lever. I placed the coin on the trolley. It annoyed him. He looked at me and put the coin on the rock. 'So, did you marry her?'

I showed him a picture of my two handsome sons—aged seven and five. He looked happy. The first time I saw him smile. He showed me a picture of his daughter, six, kept safe in a rusty, blue-coloured box on the trolley. He kept his valuables in the box, and the money under a tattered piece of cloth covering the trolley.

'She is pretty.' I smiled back.

'Like her mother,' he said.

'It feels good to smile,' I replied.

In that moment, I was less annoyed with myself. We were equals—two men in love.

I thought of the day I got married to her. She made for a lovely bride.

'Life was simple in those days,' I said. I thought of the other water seller, the other life. I couldn't recall his name, I couldn't remember asking him either.

The rules of falling in love and forging friendships were uncomplicated. I would have never befriended a water seller. Those were different times.

Gopal stayed withdrawn, wooing him was a tough job. I was the estranged lover in this relationship, nudging and praying for attention.

'For the three weeks after I saw her, I stood outside her hostel each day, paying for the glasses of water she had. *She let me.* We never spoke. She'd return from the field, having lost or won a match—it was difficult to tell. She always spoke excitedly. It cost 25 paisa back then. That water seller spoke and smiled, often. He greeted each one of us. I returned the greeting, but I didn't know anything about him. Did he have a family, a daughter, a son? I would not know. Does he still sell water? How much does he charge now? I would never know. I never went back to see him. Love in those days was pure, just like your water, Gopal.'

Gopal nodded. He looked my age, or was maybe younger. He was a handsome man.

We were communicating.

It didn't take Gopal as long as three weeks to declare his love for his wife.

'The night of our marriage, she cooked me a meal and I fell in love. It was also the first time we spoke to each other. She asked me what I did for a living. "I sell water," I replied. She laughed, gently, "In the city, people pay to buy water?" In her village, they always drank from the river. When the river dried up, they dug a well. She asked me if there was a well in the city, and I said I was yet to see one. "So, where do you get the water from?" I told her it was filtered and licensed water that I purchased from a supplier in the oldest part of town. "You pay to buy water and then sell it?" She laughed gently again, "You use chemicals to purify it?"'

Gopal was muscular and I was positive that his wife found him fine looking, but I didn't tell him so. I wondered if Gopal too came from a village. I wanted to ask him for how long he'd been selling water, why he moved his trolley outside the hospital, did he make enough money to send his daughter to school, but mostly, why was he always withdrawn. But, I knew I was not to ask questions. Soon, I would know why he didn't keep the money in the box that held his valuables. I wondered what else lay in that box. I was to learn that he was a family man and he understood his *valuables.*

He was also a man of prayers, perhaps saving his words for the little prayers he made up. He wore a *tilaka* on his forehead, sometimes. His wife had also wanted to know if there was a temple in the city, and he had taken her to one. Whenever he had the chance of a breather during his work, he'd close his eyes and mutter. I still don't know if he was religious. I never saw him pray to an idol or chant a hymn. I assumed his parents prayed to Lord Krishna. Gopal was another name for the God.

I think he prayed because his wife believed in the power of prayers. I wondered what he prayed for. He seemed so content, lacking ambition.

On the sixth day, I asked if I could join him in prayer. He let me, without asking whether I had a God, greed, creed, or need. He asked me to close my eyes and say a prayer. When I told him I'd never prayed and didn't know how to, he simply asked me to express my gratitude towards anything that made the day wonderful. I thanked God for the sun. I looked at the tree; there was no fresh sprouting, but the leaves were not droopy today.

The next day, I offered to help Gopal with his work, yet again. He told me I was a slow learner.

'I make myself coffee every morning, almost the same way. Instead of pushing the lever, I press a button,' I said in defence.

Gopal didn't look impressed. Yet, he let me fill up the glasses, count the money and wash up. 'Do you know how to squeeze a lemon?' he asked the day after. I nodded.

I don't know why he let me help; maybe he wanted me to stay mum, so that he could enjoy some quiet time. He didn't even ask me more about my wife, my boys. But I knew he cared, because his face wore a worried look on the days I got late, though he never mentioned it. He never asked me what I did for a living. I'm sure he wondered how I could afford to spend hours counting dead pinnate leaves, talk endlessly and gawk awkwardly, while he worked so hard to make ends meet. He just let me visit him each day.

On the ninth day, the skies opened up again and we got rain in abundance.

Watching me *drown*, Gopal decided to make a conversation. 'My wife loves dancing in the rain, so I like the downpours. She even loves paper boats,' he said, pointing to the one floating in a puddle near the trolley. He handed me a sheet of newspaper to try my hands on one. I made a rickety structure, which he put next to the one his wife had made.

On returning home, I taught my boys to make paper boats. I slept in my living room that night.

The next noon, when he saw me walk out of the parking lot, he said, 'If you don't like your room then sleep in your car.'

I told him I'd now be sleeping at home. He looked relieved. The same day, I offered to take home his pale, plaid shirt and wash it for him. The rain water had made its presence felt, and he'd had a long day. A VIP cavalcade was stationed inside the hospital gates. Gopal made ₹230 that day. He told me that the drivers, peons and assistants, who'd gathered around his trolley had spoken of a relief fund to be announced for those who had *suffered* the rains. Later, the newspapers confirmed the news.

When I arrived with his shirt, he seemed disinterested in my feat. He spoke of the previous day's business—the number of glasses served and broken and nimbu paani vs. water consumed. At the end of the day, he said, 'My daughter would like the smell of a clean shirt.'

I managed a smile, 'I finally learnt how to do the laundry.'

He said, 'You just had to press a button, right?'

I didn't answer.

'Tomorrow, a bunch of kids will stage a play here. It'll be busy,' he said pointing towards the ground behind the tree.

I wasn't a slow learner. I realised he needed me, so I reached the spot early. He was sweeping the ground. I began to dust his trolley, diligently. He looked annoyed and asked me to stop, 'The play is in English. I want you to narrate it to me in Hindi.' I felt very small. The children enacted ways of offering first-aid in medical emergencies. They handed over pamphlets to the audience featuring the helpline numbers of a few government authorities that sought to help flood victims.

That same evening, to make up for my ignorance, I arranged the glasses in the shape of a pyramid for him. I told him that last year I'd taken my kids to Egypt and we'd seen the Pyramids. I showed him a few pictures of the trip that were on my mobile. He asked me whether that was where I learnt how to make a pyramid of glasses.

'No,' I said, 'I learnt it at a party in the city itself, where they served Champagne. Do you know what Champagne is?'

This time too, he looked up at me and at the pyramid and said, 'City men like you might get attracted to my trolley now.'

I suggested he could start selling cola bottles too. He scoffed at the idea.

It was the day of the high tide, but Gopal began to talk about how lovely the beach was, compelling me to answer his questions.

I told him that my wife loved the beach; we often drove down and sat there for hours, while the kids made sand castles. We'd hold hands, watch the sunset, and joke about how water had brought us together. We'd celebrate by drinking fresh coconut water. On the beach, a bunch of kids were playing volleyball, a sport she gave up playing after we married. She said she needed more time to make a home, a family, and both were lovely. I missed seeing her in sports gear, though. Now, she dressed mostly in traditional Indian wear. She looked as pretty as she did back then, and said she was as comfortable in a salwar-kameez as in a pair of shorts. Her trophies from school and college were displayed in our living room, and I often told our boys that they belonged to their mom. She cooked us lovely meals, and was a perfect wife and mother.

She was like water, blending herself into my life, our lives.

I often wondered if she ever looked back at her days spent on the sports field. Or were the boys, the home and I enough to keep her happy? I thought of the times when she watched a game on television, changing channels when anyone walked into the room or how from the kitchen window she looked at the kids playing in the community park. And I wondered why she never spoke about it. Did I nudge her enough, seeking answers?

'My wife soaks her feet in the beach water, but misses the village pond,' Gopal was saying. 'In her village, they shared the water from their pond with the dwellers in the next village, and also their buffaloes. My wife disliked the city beach; flowing amidst the water were cans of cola, wrappers of candies and wafers, broken chappals, cigarette butts, corncobs and dog poop.'

Did I know what Sona, my wife, disliked? Very hot tea that couldn't hold the biscuit beyond two seconds, radio stations that played many advertisements and yes, sugar-free desserts. Did I know what she missed, regretted? Perhaps, I did. Did we ever speak about it, openly? Perhaps not. On the 13th day, I brought prasad for Gopal and his family. He took it with folded hands. He didn't ask me a single question. 'Take some home for your wife and daughter, and tell them I'll visit them soon.'

He didn't look up, but I was not in a mood to nudge. I sat on the rock, eating the prasad. 'Extra sugar, please,' I could hear Sona say.

'My daughter will love it,' Gopal said, looking at the halwa and puri still in his hands.

He opened his rusty blue box and brought out a picture of his wife. In the same box was a newspaper clipping of the city floods that had claimed 250 lives in a slum, less than a fortnight ago. He ran a finger down the names of the deceased, stopping at a name he'd underlined—Chiti.

Chiti meant love or beloved.

There was a marigold in the box too.

'Today was my wife's *tehravin*,' he said. 'But please do come sometime and meet my daughter; she's a lovely girl, just like her mother.'

My throat was now parched. I couldn't even bear to look at him.

And just like that, it became *our* story.

I was, indeed, the estranged lover, unaware of his pain.

It was a day we spent in silence.

And as the sun set, I realised it was time for me to get back to my life. It was time to start looking after our boys, return to work and sleep on our bed.

It was time to learn how to grieve and miss, and yet live.

It was time to celebrate Sona's life, our love.

I just hoped it was not too late.

***

I spent those 13 days in the shade of a limp coconut tree. Gopal and I both lost our wives in the city floods. They both breathed their last behind the tall iron gates, in the hospital. Sona was in a private ward, Chiti in the general. Sona lived in a city apartment, Chiti in a *jhuggi*.

Nature doesn't distinguish.

Gopal calmed many lives and parched throats. I stared at the gates seeking answers and cursing life. Gopal was a content man, lacking ambition.

We were equals—two men remembering our loves.

I was yet to learn, I was yet to pay tribute.

Gopal was my teacher, my friend.

*****

HANDSOME POINT

Just like with many other little boys, my first hairstyle icon was my dad. I'd watch him comb his hair with a small, white, plastic comb, the tines working their magic on his hair from front to back. Once done, he'd keep the comb in the back pocket of his trousers and get going with the day. The comb would appear again once or twice daily, performing the same function.

I'd tell him, 'Daddy, you have lovely hair,' and he'd sprinkle a few drops of water on my head and style my hair too.

'You're such a handsome boy,' he'd say, and I'd walk up to my mother and tell her he'd said so.

I was happy with my hairdresser. But the year I turned five, Dad announced it was time for me to have a haircut. 'We'll be visiting the barber,' he said. It made me very upset.

The barber shop, offering only three services: haircut, shave and massage, was housed in the shade of a gulmohar tree with a fissured, shallowly cracked bark.

On my first visit to the barber shop, I wailed sitting in my dad's lap, 'The scissors are scary and sharp.'

To keep me still and engaged, Dad told the story of a horse that could turn into an airplane. He held my attention and I had my first haircut. When I returned home, though I was happy with the image in the mirror, I felt thankful—the ordeal was over. But I was wrong. Twenty-five days later, Dad announced it was time for another trip to the barber.

'Dad, why do I need to go again?'

'Because a man has to be regular with his haircuts.'

This time around, I sat on a wooden plank placed between the arms of the barber's chair, with my legs dangling.

'You're a big boy now,' Dad said, as he helped me onto the wooden plank.

I didn't cry; I was still and quiet. He stood next to me as I held his hand, clenching it each time the scissors was in my view. The third visit happened sooner than I'd hoped. Dad sat on a wooden bench behind the barber chair and read a newspaper. I was on my own. I settled down calmly and the barber narrated the tale of the magical horse that turned into an airplane. I was surprised he knew the story too. I noticed my dad's smiling reflection in the long mirror with the dark-green plastic frame in front of me.

I knew my numbers, so I began to read the ones on the calendar that hung next to the mirror.

It was the year 1983, but the calendar read '1981'. I don't think the outdated calendar bothered anyone. The calendar, dotted with yellow spots and punctured at many dates, was certainly not there to keep track of time. And then anyone who wished to keep up with the times was to be seen at hair salons, not barber shops; I was to learn that later.

Sundar was always dressed in a white vest and pants, both clean, with his gold chain sitting on his chest, perhaps his most valuable possession. On days when the sun shone, the gold would glimmer in the mirror and I would chase the reflection as it fell on it, the floor and the chair. Next to his feet, lay a crumpled plastic bottle filled with water that he picked up each time he needed to wet the hair. A bulky white plastic bag holding squeezed and fresh tubes of shaving creams and lotions lay next to it.

The leaves of the calendar were rarely turned, but the months and years were passing by, for soon enough I was sitting on the chair and the wooden plank was gone—the latter was only for kids. And just like that, over a few dozen haircuts, my dad's barber, Sundar, had become mine too, and a tradition was passed down.

The chair where I had my first cut is still there, but its red fabric is peeling off in many places. The lever for adjusting its height has long gone, with no prospect of being replaced; bricks work just as well. The once dark-green frame that outlined the mirror is now pale and chipped, with strips of masking tape covering the cracks. The number of black spots on the mirror grew as my height did, rapidly and then slowly. The shop bears no brand endorsements, or perhaps it needs no brand identity, for 'sundar' itself means beautiful. It carries no signage of product trademarks. It offers the same three services with no plans of making any addition.

Sundar still trusts his old pair of scissors the most, occasionally using two new stainless steel ones—a pointed one that he uses with a comb or his fingers to chop to chosen lengths, and the thinning shears that remove approximately half the hair passed through it. Sundar's hands tremble now as he parts my hair. He's 68. Yet, I keep returning for cuts under the shade of the tree and a blue plastic canopy. Sundar and I both know that the days of traditional barber shops housed under trees are numbered; modern salons in air-conditioned rooms are a looming threat. But a handful of us continue to have our hair cut by the old barbers in such dying shops, refusing to change. I wonder why; why do I never miss my dates with Sundar or change my barber? Why do I keep returning regularly to Sundar's makeshift barber shop, Handsome Point?

I recall my father telling me, 'This shop is older than Sundar. Sundar simply took over when his father died. He didn't shed a tear or share the news with the customers. The day his father died, the barber shops in the neighbourhood remained closed as a mark of respect, while the salons continued to do business. With his head shaved, he stood at the same spot his father had every day for nine hours. His father never took a day off, the shop was always open, and Sundar couldn't let that change. He didn't allow himself a mourning period. A day was all he took to both grieve and perform the last rites at his father's funeral. He simply continued the work of his father. Visiting the shop a fortnight later, I noticed that Sundar had placed a picture of his father at the heart of a display featuring Bollywood heroes with simple and stylish hair trends, all pasted onto the tree. Sundar was smiling and consoling as he did the *mundan* of a one-year-old boy. I observed it didn't take him long to win the trust of his father's clients. Old-school barbers aren't trained at school, they just learn by watching their fathers and grandfathers. When one of his father's oldest customers sat in the chair, he wore a sense of confidence. I watched Sundar use his fingers to create a parting in his hair, a few inches off-centre, just like his father had.'

Sundar always remembers everyone's hair textures, partings, types, patterns, and sideburns. 'Like elephants, barbers never forget.'

And on that point, Dad was right. In my college years, I'd done with various radical appearances: volume at the front, length on top, sides slicked with tapered back. And when I told Sundar I wanted to return to the original, he knew instantly what to do. And I wasn't the only one walking up to the shop and asking for 'the usual'. Over the years, I noticed how boys (with few exceptions) started out happy experimenting with their hair, then, as they grew up, they became happier reverting to their original styles and sticking with them. 'You can change partners, but not your barber,' I heard a 65-year-old man with short hair at the sides, longer hair on top and an undefined parting say.

Old-school barbers charge little for a cut, they don't distinguish between who sits on their chair. The men's only spot is not defined by any kind of boundaries either; if not on the bench, you can stand beside it or sit atop the rocks next to it.

Handsome Point is always full, and you can usually get a cut, shave or massage without an appointment, and everyone talks here as they wait.

I find it tough to let go of this habit of sitting in this chair, which by the way, now looks like a cross between a dentist's chair, a throne and a wheelchair. And I know exactly why, for as I wait for my turn and read the newspaper, just like my dad did, I am reminded of the two times when I nakedly cried and let myself feel weak in Sundar's chair, amidst a bunch of men, known and unknown.

Last year, when I lost my dad and shared the news with Sundar, he hugged me, briefly and warmly. I felt a tear roll down my face. I wasn't ashamed to cry in front of him. He let me cry as freely as I had on my first visit at the age of five. At 36, sitting in his chair, grieving, I drew comfort from the memories and images of my younger days when Dad and I would walk up to the shop together. It was our time—father and son, man to man. I thought how much I'd grown up between my first haircut and first shave, and how much I'd miss watching Dad's reflection as he sat on the barber's bench. I'd become a man; he'd grown old and lost most of his hair. I'd moved from my parents' home long ago, but each time it was time to walk to the barber shop, I'd call Dad and check to see if he needed a cut too. He always agreed to show up, irrespective of whether he needed a service, saying, 'Real men go to barber shops, not salons.'

It's on these visits during weak and other moments that I feel manlier—perhaps it is the combination of the smell of hair oil and shaving foam; maybe it's the shop's mirror that reflects my pride at the new growth of hair on my chin and my experiments with hair during the growing-up years; or could it just be that Sundar's chair is one of the few places I have a chance to think and talk clearly.

I walk into the spot, alone now. Yet, I feel I am not on my own. I join in the cheering and sighing over a cricket commentary from the old transistor. For years, the transistor has stood on a small table holding Sundar's tools: clippers, single-razor blades, combs, neck dusters, water spray bottles, etc. Between scissor clicks, all subjects are aired: share markets, anniversary gifts, office promotions, partner habits, holiday plans, job offers, income tax returns and internet download speeds.

Handsome Point is a place I look forward to visiting; it's what we call 'A round table of wise men'.

There's no doubt that the comfort of sitting in the chair of a barber familiar with the many contours of your head and complexities of your hair is unmatchable. The anxiety of sitting in a new chair is one that I dread, in common with all the men who wait patiently on the rugged bench for their turn. When a new family moved to the neighbourhood, I remember the anxiety of the father leaving behind his old barber. I recommended Sundar, and he finally agreed to go to him once I'd said my father and I had been going to the same shop for years. I asked Sundar to look after this new neighbour when I went for my next regular cut and shave.

'He shifted here three months back. He works in a bank and has two lovely boys,' I told him. 'He's been to the hair salon across the road thrice; each time a different hairdresser cut his hair and he didn't like that.'

My neighbour became a regular at Sundar's. As my dad would say, 'Every man needs a reliable and skilled barber.' I knew what he meant. Sundar would always understand exactly what I meant each time I said 'a little off the sides'. He gives everyone the cut they ask for. Many men with receding hairlines and bald patches sit in his chair; he chops his scissors in the air every time and tells them, 'all is not lost'.

'Do all men talk in your chair?' I asked Sundar one day. He thought for a while and said, 'Sixty per cent of them talk, 40 per cent think.'

It's easy to talk in that chair. I myself had spoken to him about airplanes, homework and friends.

'When do you start work?' he asked when I found a job.

When my wife had our first child, a daughter, it was in his chair that I acknowledged my fears, 'I don't know how to be a dad to my little girl.' But I was certain of one thing that when years later she'd bring home a man she would want to marry, I'll ask him about his years of association with his barber. I told this to Sundar and we had a good laugh. Men need traditions to help them bond, another lesson I learnt from my dad.

At his shop, under the open skies, we grumble over hair partings and games lost, complain about extra inches cut and partial hair loss, and openly share the pain of razor cuts and broken hearts. But there's more to my visits than conditioners, conversations and clippers.

The shop hasn't changed with cultural or generational shifts; it still offers a straightforward experience and a sense of continuity. Sundar never lures his customers with fancy offers or discounts; his rate list stays glued to the tree trunk, as ever. Over the years, he's never even bothered to paste up a new rate list, and merely uses a ballpoint pen to replace the old rates with the new ones. The rate card does more than document inflation; it also shows rises and falls, births and deaths—the circle of life.

The sense of permanence prevails.

I wonder if Sundar ever walks by the new-age salons with their school-trained staff and looks at the word 'WELCOME' etched on their glass doors, worrying if it will soon be time for him to put his scissors to rest, comparing his worth in money and otherwise, whether he succeeds in defending his profession to his son, if he ever regrets continuing the tradition of the low caste, the barbers' clan.

Last week, as Sundar gave me a straight razor shave (another service that could die out with the old-school barber), I asked him so, 'Just a few men wait on your bench for their turn. Are they enough to run your home? Until when do you think these days will last?'

'For a long time to come,' he said. 'After all, you can't trust anyone to hold a razor to your neck.' And we both laughed as he fixed the adjustable neck rest for shaving.

As I walked back home, I recalled my dad's words: 'A good barber is for keeps.'

Yes, the rest of the world might have changed and moved on to air-conditioned salons, appointment diaries, electric clippers, professional stylists and hair dressers, but I haven't, because after all 'Real men go to barber's shops, not salons.'

I reach home and sprinkle a few drops of water on my son's hair and style it for him, with my small white comb. We were blessed with him two years ago.

'Soon it will be time for your first haircut at the barber's shop,' I tell him, as he crawls on the floor. 'Because that's where the real men go.'

*****

BETWEEN US, DAUGHTER AND MOTHER

My mum never told me I had a vagina; in fact, neither did my sisters, aunts or nanny.

We, three sisters, were told we each had two arms and two legs, a face, head, back and stomach, and that's about it. Mum and the aunts never stopped us from asking questions, but they never answered all our questions.

When one morning my nanny was giving me a bath and I asked her what to call my nipples, she smiled sheepishly, but didn't answer. The next day at bath time, when

I asked her what to call my vagina, she became very upset with me. She told Mum that I was learning wrong things at school and that Mum needed to keep a close watch on what I was being taught.

I was six and honestly wasn't really learning much at school. I wanted to tell that to Nanny. My recent learning included how to write five-letter words, add and subtract double-digit numbers, and mix red and blue on the palette to make purple. The rest of the time, I played at school: in the grounds, the classroom and the swing area. But I'd clearly upset my nanny. From the next day onwards, she started to give me hurried showers without bothering to check if the water was too hot or too cold. Once done, she'd briskly rub me with a towel and ask me to put on my underpants and vest, all by myself. It made me very upset. I was too scared to ask which the correct sides of the garments were and many times, I wore them inside out. No one at school noticed; the private garments were hidden under my uniform.

When my mum took notice of that, she decided to have a little chat with me. 'Nanny must have complained about my bad behaviour,' I thought to myself as Mum helped me identify my clothes the right way round.

'Look for the label that says "Tinker Bell", she should always sit on your backside,' said Mum, fixing my clothes.

'Did I upset Nanny?' I asked her.

Mum smiled at me warmly and said, 'Oh, you know how hard she works. And when naughty children like you ask her too many questions, she acts funny.'

That same week, Mum taught me how to shower by myself. 'Clean yourself properly, everywhere, even down there,' she said.

But she didn't tell me what to call *it*.

I was smart, I got the message. Just like I was not to ask for a third helping of ice cream, I was to not ask what *it* was called.

For a long time, I was sure that Mum didn't know the answer either.

When I reached grade five and our science teacher took us through the chapter Parts of the Human Body, she showed us a chart that had every part labelled, except *it*. Maybe *it* didn't have a name. I had a head and toes, neck and knees, and a small and large intestine in between.

And then, I thought that if my teacher and Mum didn't know, how could anyone else possibly do?

I learnt not to ask questions. I learnt not to bother over what lay down there.

But the same year everything changed and I found all my answers one evening; I bled heavily that day.

Honestly, I'm not sure if I should tell you everything that happened that evening. My mum won't like it, for sure. My nanny will probably stop working in our house. My sisters will be very upset. My friends will be told not to wear certain kinds of clothes. My brother and dad will both feel embarrassed and ashamed. But then, I don't think I can hide it because when the sun rises, everyone will know this story, *my story*.

Certain people will tell imaginary tales about how it must have happened. A few women will shed tears, a few men will be angry. Perhaps someone will call the police and I'll be laid down onto the ground, and then a phone call will be made to you, Mum. After that moment, I'll be public news; nothing more will be just between you and me, Mum. The incident will be there in the newspapers and on TV news channels. Maybe they'll protect my name.

Maybe they'll give me another name. Maybe they'll call me names. But in the middle of all of this, Mum, I'm afraid you'll miss the last words I want to say to you. Because, Mum, in the middle of all the protests, the punishment seeking, the candle-lit marches, the screenplays and the campaigns, they'll find another girl hanging from a tree. And just like that, I'll be old news—forgotten.

I'm telling you this story because I know you won't be able to gather the courage to walk up to the tree and look at me. I know you'll cry and scream in pain and anger, and ask yourself why no one ever told you what *it* was called and hence, why you could never tell me I had a vagina. I know you will blame yourself for not being able to protect your little princess. But Mum, I want to tell you that I know you taught me all that you knew, all that Granny and aunts taught you. I know you were a good mother, and raised me well.

Mum, it happened on that lovely windy day. Remember? I walked up to you and told you how much I loved the breeze. 'I love it even when it blows the flower in my hair in the wrong direction, or carries my umbrella away. I always try to feel its rhythm and sing along. We're friends.' You laughed and told me I could write a love poem for the breeze.

Mum, I never feared the breeze. We got along in all seasons, I told you so. So why did it betray me? Why did it turn against me? Why did we stop being friends?

That evening, I wore the polka dot frock you bought me for my 10th birthday. It was a cheerful lime-green and a happy white. Remember? I slipped into it the moment you took it out from the brown paper bag. I still remember the sound the bag made when I jumped and took it from your hands. It made me smile. I loved it.

I'd grown just half an inch taller, but the dress still fell over my knees. I wore it to a friend's birthday in the neighbourhood. I had lovely chocolate cake with choco-chips at the party. You'd told me to be home on time, so I left at six o'clock. Her house was just three houses away from ours. I should have been home in the next five minutes.

But Mum, as I walked back home, the breeze made my dress flutter. It couldn't cover my knees any more.

I saw four men—tall, bald, old and young. They were a cheerful bunch of uncles. I think they too were returning from a birthday party. They were laughing loudly, and teasing the youngest. The oldest man was holding a brown-tinted glass bottle in his hand. I couldn't hear the joke, but it made me smile. It was a lovely day, the breeze was magical.

I was almost home, just across the parking lot, when the men came up to me.

I remembered your words from when I was seven. That time, I had helped an old man walk up the stairs. 'Don't be silly, stopping and talking to strangers.'

They said something to me; I didn't answer. I couldn't even hear them properly and simply walked faster into our apartment gates. Just then, the bald man grabbed me by my hand. I asked him to leave me alone, politely at first. Then he tightened his grip. I jerked his hand with all my strength.

Mum, he was very strong. I called for the security guard at the gate to help; he stood up, looked at me and walked off in the opposite direction. The bald man waved at the guard, then covered my face with a dirty piece of cloth; it smelt of sweat. I think the bald man and the guard were friends. The bald man then dragged me by my hair.

I could see your reflection in the kitchen window as you made dinner. I could see the fairy lights in my room twinkling, waiting for my return. I could see Dad's empty parking spot; he wasn't home yet. I could see my brother's room, dark. I remember you telling him to be home on time, by ten o'clock. I could see my younger sister watching the television and my eldest sister playing with her mobile. I could see my home.

I was almost home on time, Mum, 6:03 pm.

I remembered your words: 'If you want to go to the other birthday party next week, be home by six in the evening.'

The bald man lifted me up and threw me over his shoulder. 'She's making a lot of noise,' the old man had said, pointing at my feet. As he walked, I kept pulling my dress down.

I remembered your words: 'What are they teaching you at school? Stand properly, you're a grown-up now. Don't let your underpants show.'

But Mum, the way he held me, I couldn't do much. I shifted positions every few seconds, trying to free myself from him, but each time he slapped me hard on the hips. He walked a few steps ahead of the other three men, then suddenly dropped me on the ground.

I yelped with pain as my head hit the trunk of a tree.

The bald man asked me to shut up. I continued to weep, softly. He bent down and started to kiss me. I was shocked. I was confused. I wept.

I remembered your words, last summer, when I told you Dad's friend, Uncle, had kissed me: 'It's a secret,' you'd said. You asked me to not tell anyone.

The bald man then said to the old man, 'Maybe you can shut her up?'

As the old man pressed his mouth against my cheeks, my neck and my lips, I tried to see where I was.

Remember the tree behind the parking lot, where the street light hasn't worked for the last five months? The one that Dad looks at, and says, 'I wonder when the municipality will repair that?'

I was under that tree.

Then I screamed loudly. I called for you and Dad many times. I tried to stand up and run, but the bald man pushed me down. I was now barefoot; I think my left shoe came off when he lifted me up near the gate. I hoped when you came looking, my shoe would show you the way to me, like in *Hansel and Gretel.* Or maybe you'd find my hair clips; their tiny stones shining in the dark. It was a winter evening. The sun had gone home.

The men didn't like it when I screamed again, so the bald man asked the youngest man to stuff my right shoe into my mouth.

Mum, I was very confused. Why did he do that? Were they going to hit me? Why had they got me here?

There was no one to answer my questions, just like when I was little.

The breeze was now blowing fiercely, and the branches of the tree shook violently. Both made a lot of noise. Now my screams wouldn't reach you.

I was lying on many twigs, leaves and broken branches.

The tall man picked up a stick and lifted my dress. I protested with my hands. He stood on them, and told the bald man to rip my dress off. They didn't unzip it from behind, but tore it apart, laughing loudly. I was now in my underpants and Barbie vest.

The bald man cackled, 'She's for you, my child,' as he threw my vest towards the youngest man.

I began to howl. The bald man slapped me very hard, on my face. I cried louder with my stuffed mouth; it made him angry. He ripped away my underpants; they fell near my feet.

I remembered your scolding, that time I told you Dad's friend, Uncle, had asked me to show him my underpants: 'Don't be stupid, go inside and change your clothes.'

Mum, I was so ashamed to be naked. I hope you can believe me.

The old man announced he would go first. Everyone cheered for him. I wasn't sure what would happen. The next thing I knew, he'd taken off his clothes and was standing above me. He hurt me down there. He pinched my nipples. He asked me if I was having fun. He said he was.

Then Mum, they took turns to hurt me. They wanted to share me, they said.

I remembered your words: 'Sharing is caring.' You'd said sharing was a good thing. As they joked and decided what order they'd have me in, I thought of the poem you helped me write when I was eight: 'We share because we care'. We never used the word 'pain' in that poem.

I was in pain and they were making me swallow something; it tasted awful. Then one of the men picked up a broken stump of wood and pushed the sharp end down there. I could feel the blood running. I couldn't keep my eyes open. I felt like I was about to faint. I wanted to sleep. I was done in.

I remembered your words: 'Why are you jumping over the gates? Let your brother reach first, you take the long route, walk with me.'

Mum, I can't be sure how long they laughed at me, put things inside me, licked me, kissed me and splashed stuff on my chest and face.

I don't even know when I started to run out of breath. I think it was somewhere between the tall man spitting on me and telling the youngest one that he needed to learn the ways to own a woman. He giggled like he'd been handed a toy to play with. He played with me for a long time—feeling me everywhere. He imitated what he'd seen the older men do. He rolled me—front and then, back. The tall man handed him sticks and challenged him to push them inside me. There was cheering as he did so.

My eyes were now almost shut, but I could see the tree above me; it was huge. The green spread covered the whole sky above it and also what happened beneath. I couldn't see the stars. The breeze was shaking the branches—its many branches. You do remember the tree, don't you, Mum?

And then the old man said, 'Let's hang her up on that branch,' as he savoured the last drop of the liquid from the brown-tinted bottle and smashed the bottle to the ground. It was very dark. 'Come on, who's going to give me a hand?' I think the fact that both the liquid and I were finished, made him angry. He lifted a shard from the broken glass bottle and tried to stab my navel. In the darkness, he missed the first couple of times, which made him angrier. Then he dragged me closer to the tree trunk and began to climb the tree. He was a strong man; he'd reach the branch in no time.

By now I knew I was dying. I knew people could and did die. I'd read about it in *Sleeping Beauty*. The bad fairy, angry from being overlooked, placed a spell on the princess; she'd prick her hand on a spindle and die. I knew there was no good fairy around, to reverse the evil curse.

But I wondered why they wanted to hang me on the tree. Then the old man said, 'This is your prize,' to the young one. The young and the bald men lifted me high enough to reach the branch; they seemed delighted with their work. I wasn't pretty any more—the kohl you'd let me put on for the party had smudged. I know that mixing black and red can never make a pleasant shade. As I'd cried, the kohl had flown down with the tears to meet the blood on my upper lip.

The old man pulled me up with his big hands and using my polka dot dress tied my hands around the branch. The knot was weak, but it held me there, dangling, till the sun's rays fell, showing everyone the 'prize'.

And then a few seconds later, everything stopped hurting.

The tears stopped, the pain vanished and the men left.

The last time I looked down at myself, at the ground and down there, I remembered your words from the last time I had asked you what to call *it*: 'I don't know what *it's* called. Don't ask me or anyone else.'

Mum, I wish you'd told me what *it* was and what they could do to *it*.

Mum, I wish you'd told me why it was *really unsafe* for girls to be out till late; because there are evil men lurking on the streets, ready to pounce.

Mum, I wish you'd told me why my underpants shouldn't be seen; because there are men waiting to rip them apart.

Mum, I wish you'd told me why I shouldn't jump over the gates; because the spokes could hurt me down there.

Mum, I wish you'd told me why I should stay quiet about Dad's friend, Uncle, kissing me; because you felt as weak and helpless as I did that evening.

Mum, I wish you'd told me I had a vagina.

Mum, I wish you'd tell my sisters what *it* is.

Mum, I wish Granny had told you so.

Mum, I wish you knew all this.

But Mum, don't blame Granny. May be her mother too didn't know that little girls can be hurt down there; maybe she too thought that her dad's friends, all the uncles, were nice men.

Mum, I wish you'd remember that I know you loved me a lot and I too loved you to the moon and back.

Mum, I wish both you and I knew there was a word for what I had down there, vagina, and it was not a bad word.

Mum, I wish we both had found answers to our questions.

Mum, I wish you'd always know in your heart that I was happy to be your daughter.

Mum, I wish you'd know that this was not how I wanted to say goodbye.

Mum, I wish you find the courage to hold me in your arms and bid me a loving farewell.

***

I was raped and killed under a baobab tree—the newspapers reported so. I was 11.

Last week, my dad complained about the faulty street light again.

I can tell you my name; then again, it's hard to remember names, right?

The public memory is very short.

*****

THE PLAYER

I judge rich married women by their acne and attitude, scent and status, flab and fashion, wealth and worth. I like them, too; but not all. I'm partial to a certain kind. Everyone has their favourites. Me, I like rich married women who are eager to cheat on their partners. I don't distinguish between them—they're equals. As for their partners, I have nothing to do with them. This game I play needs just two participants, and no bystanders. It's played between a lady and her presswallah.

Before you raise your brows and begin to wonder what they're doing with me, take a look. I'm hard to resist.

That oblong face, angular jaw line, slightly curved chin and scruffy stubble; it's tricky to imagine a more charming consort. And on the days I wear my long crop back on my face, it's checkmate. But wait! Don't mistake me for a Casanova. I'm a player, and there's a fine line between the two. I don't fear commitment, but I'm not in the game to make or break relationships. Yes, I seek passion, but my scope isn't limited to the bedroom.

I use my charm to bring me all I crave—the wealth of the diamonds and the pleasures of the bed. I want to taste everything that the rich have, not just their women. And I carry no arrogance. I know that without the women, I'd have never gained entry into the empires of the rich. And I am a realist too. I know vanity doesn't last forever. No game goes on forever, for now age is on my side and I know I have to play exhaustively till it lasts.

I give these women what they want, and accept what they give. Some offer me pearls, others, afternoons of lust. A few let me wear their husband's suits, many ache and plead to be touched. And I never say no. I indulge in the erotic enjoyments and idealistic involvements, enjoying each conquest as if it were my first and last. But there's one rule I never let the women forget—in this game, I'm the man.

I turn 27 this year, and in my 12 years of playing the game, there's never been a time when I've allowed that rule to be overlooked, even in my first conquest, at 15. That year is one I distinctly remember. It was when I first recognised my urge to *grow*. I was sitting on the marble floor of a glitzy house, waiting to collect a bundle of clothes I'd be ironing later in the day. At 15, this was my only skill; the one I picked up from a man with a broken heart.

The floor gleamed like a mirror and it caught my reflection—smooth skin on the smooth floor. I sat gazing at the satin drapes, dreaming how it would feel to smooth out their creases. The charcoal in my iron would warm up and my sturdy, brown hands would exert just the right amount of pressure on the fabric to make the wrinkles vanish. I was lost in my thoughts when the lady of the house walked past me. She caught my attention with the carats on her fingers, the silk on her body and the red on her lips. I caught hers with the fresh sprouting of hair on my chest, the ease with which I sat, legs wide apart, and the frailness of my slim waist.

I heard my feeble voice saying, 'Can I touch the satin drapes, please?'

She bent down, revealing the space between her breasts, speaking to me. She ran a hand across my bare chest, then reached down to my thighs, stopping where they met. 'Yes, you can,' she said and left.

The next day, when I took back the clean, fresh-smelling pile of clothes, she gave me a piece of shiny red satin.

'I'll clean it and iron it well,' I heard my unruffled voice saying.

'It's a prize, a cravat. Wear it round your neck.' She smiled and left.

I didn't sleep well that night. Holding the red satin close to my chest, I could smell the richness. The velvet, the satin and the silk, could be all mine. I dreamt that life. And that's how I became a player—the presswallah who flattened the wrinkles in garments and bed sheets, gawping at the realms of wealth; the presswallah who turned a blind eye to the wrinkles that showed on skin: white, black or brown.

My 15th year was significant for another reason. It was the year I began to resist the temptation to curse my mother. My charm and craft was her offering to me.

I knew nothing of her, but I'd heard stories of her debauchery—a colourful, attractive, fearless woman. I'm told I was the result of a night of passion; a child was not part of her game, so she abandoned me under a banyan tree and moved on to *sin* again. She left me wailing, and soon after, as just a three-month-old, I began to be known as the poor boy who fed on the leftovers of the rich.

My moist and innocent eyes, and sharp mind and charming looks were destined to earn me shelter from the poor, paltry jobs from the middle class and fortunes from the rich.

A laundry man who was besotted with my mother, took me into his care in the hope that I'd act as bait to bring her back to his bed and perhaps, life. Over the years, as he let me sleep in his bed, I grew to pity him. He struggled on, in the belief that my mother knew how to love. He was an ageing man, eager to be loved and bedded before it would be time to retire. I wished him all the best.

When I was 13, his wait for my mother ended and my time to move forward began. Here, under this tree, I inherited all that belonged to him. The bundles you see around me are large and small; they hold clothes in all styles, of all sizes and bear all kinds of smells. The charcoal-fired brass iron is his too, as is the table on which everything sits. I didn't want him to leave me with all he had, but in the end, I guess, we both knew it was only me he had.

He was a lazy teacher, but I was a keen student. His collection and delivery of bundles of clothes were always meticulous. He *never* lost a garment entrusted to him, burnt a cloth or left a day's business unfinished before nightfall. He was a master at ironing out folds in fabrics: soft and coarse, old and new. He visited the homes of the rich, twice a day—in the mornings to collect the bundles and in the evenings to deliver the smooth layers. He settled the bill each day, tallying his accounts before sunset.

I observed him and carried on his craft.

And like him, I always remember which pieces of cloth belong where. I've never mixed up a delivery. I work as hard as he did and perhaps, harder on some days. I've never given anyone a reason to complain and I don't keep an account book; my scores are settled before sunset.

But there's one thing I do differently. I never let love interfere with my work. I'm not in the queue, I'm ahead of the queue.

Maybe I'm like my mother, love wasn't for her too. Maybe she still lives the life that I live now. Maybe this is what she wanted for me. Why else would she abandon me under a tree in the ritziest and most conceited part of the town?

She left me here to flourish, while she flourished too. I don't think I'll see her again, but if I do, I'll tell her, 'Mother, I reciprocated every interest expressed, and I never judged what lay under the garments.'

'Is your game different from mine?' I'd ask. 'Do you fear the loss of vanity as I do and is there a trick to deceive age? If yes, then would you teach me how to master that?' And then, if she's not running late for her conquest to indulge and win, I'll tell her the way I played and what I inherited from her.

Mother, my ironing table stands under the tree where you abandoned me. I'm surrounded by the houses of clients—yours and mine. Standing here, I enjoy a clear view of the world of the rich. I see their leather couches and opulent beds. I catch the aromas of their meals on silver platters and expensive fragrances on their wrists. At times, I climb up the tree and take a closer look at their tinted glasses and plastered walls. I stay alert for the sounds of the tinkling of glasses and roaring cars. I know when the masters are away and when they're back. The women are always eager to be heard and I let them tell me their tales of pain, pleasure, greed, heartbreak, fear and desire. I don't interrupt once, nor do I hear a single word. I just sit on the cushioned bed and watch them talk. I compliment them if I feel they're aching for that, but mostly, I just let them talk.

Before I begin my day of work, I cover my big bare chest with my pale blue shirt. I don't want soot or smoke leaving a cloud of black on my giant square pecs. I know if I lose those, I'll soon have nothing left. I tread carefully and cover myself from anything evil and black.

The women have little time and are eager to pounce with a roar or grace defeat with a whimper, just after the master leaves. They are inflamed, at times emotional and irrational. I don't want the diseases of the rich, so I announce to them that I need to cover my bare self. 'If we're not careful, we'll lose whatever we have.'

When it's time to get started, I take off the top of the iron and add the charcoal inside, enough to reach the brim. As I do this, a few pieces of charcoal fall out and dirty both my hands and the sheet that's spread across the ironing table. I remove the pieces so that my customers don't complain that I fouled their belongings.

We all want a clean game, with no dirty secrets and surprises. We all deserve equal chances of winning. I never speak about their men and they're never shy about parting with their wealth. Bystanders only stink up the game.

I open the old cola bottle filled with kerosene and pour a few drops on the charcoal. I'm careful. I don't want to smell bad. With a matchstick, I light a small fire and allow it to burn for a while.

The women tell me they want to retaliate and play another game; an eye for an eye with their men. I let them play; I'm the silent accomplice. I don't appear and I don't stink.

As the iron warms up, I place the garment to be ironed on the sheet, on the ironing table. I smooth it out with my hands, and don't bring the iron close till it's ready to perform.

My sizeable beauty is eager to speak for itself. I let it wander among the beautiful, ugly, tall, puny, bony, amusing, unpleasant, rude, ridiculous, shabby and elegant. I let it lust, brazenly.

It's now time to carry the iron a little away from the table, and start blowing on the charcoal with my mouth. I fan the flame and use a small stick to mix the charcoal around, ensuring the pieces are getting hot.

My conquests are lonely at times, at others, discontent. I offer myself when I'm needed and stay for as long as I am required. I fill the empty and deprived hollow—in their showy lives and in between their legs.

A little while later, when I open the lid, I see the glowing embers of charcoal.

The player is pleased and the game draws to a slow or a sudden end. When the thirst is quenched, the women realise and remember that it's me, lying in their bed.

The iron is ready and I lift it and run it back and forth along the garments.

I remind the women that in this game, I'm the man. I ask them to hand me my clothes so I can dress up. I let them find theirs. As they use their hands to remove the creases in their outfits and the knots in their hair, I leave the scene and head back.

I iron the garments till they're crisp and wrinkle free. I fold each of them up and place one on top of the other, neatly. Every pile has space, for each piece of fabric. They're all equal.

The women are aware that they share me with their neighbours, sisters, aunts and friends. I tell each one that she's the best. I lie well.

And when the sun sets and the consignments have been delivered, I tally my accounts and rest well. Tomorrow is a new day, and the charcoal will have to be burnt again.

My pot of gold is full and the women are spent. But we are neither exhausted nor content. We wake up thirsty, imagining the adventures that lie ahead.

And Mother, the clothes I deliver are always spotless and clean. I never burn a piece of cloth, nor my hands.

Because I was borne of the wealthy.

Mother, is that why you left me to flourish among them?

*****

SCENT OF THE FAMILIAR

Our lives can often be described as a sum of certain scents: soft baby lotion, fruity shampoo, mild detergent, pleasant sheets, soothing food from Mum's kitchen, wet colour paints, time-worn pictures, dusty chalk powder, groovy cologne, moist earth, Dad's old files, smiling coffee beans, grim burnt wood, still newspaper and peaceful incense sticks.

Growing up in a home that was rich with aromatic nuances, scents began to define me from an early age. And one of the memories that I hold dearest stems from the whiff of henna leaves from my aunt's house. When the pungent aroma wafted towards me, I'd know that she'd soon be calling out to me. Restless, I'd stop colouring and stand behind the kitchen door, so I could appear as soon as I heard my name. Seconds later, I'd be standing on a small step ladder, handing little bottles and boxes from a shelf over to my aunt. Filled with pride, my aunt would later tell the neighbours how I'd helped her. Her appreciative and encouraging nods with each bottle and box made me feel like an adult. She'd then put spices, oils and tea leaves in a pan of boiling water with the henna leaves.

'Let it boil for a few hours now,' she'd say, and I'd reply, 'And cool down after that.' We knew what we were doing, we were partners.

Two days later, I'd excitedly watch her apply the blend she'd prepared. At times, a drop would fall on the floor and she'd clean it immediately, lest the blot left a mark. She had lovely long hair: black, orange and grey. I'd tell her I wanted hair like hers, and she'd say I would if I ate my greens.

Once the blend had been applied to every strand, she'd tie a piece of old cloth around her hair and prepare our lunch. When I woke up from my nap, her long hair would be loose, wet, orange and black. She'd let me comb the strands. I'd take in deep breaths and smile. It made me so happy, that sharp, familiar smell. In the evening, we'd walk down to a neighbourhood market. It was my turn to be henna'ed. She'd say, 'Mehendi for your little hands.'

We'd walk a short distance and then stop right in front of the sweet shop. In front of the shop was a row of gulmohar trees, under each tree would be sitting a man, all just a few metres away from each other. There were small benches next to each tree, each man. The men looked similar, with the same design books, the same footstools and even the same mehendi cones. They all charged the same price and made similar designs. Choosing one reminded me of the 'spot the difference' caricatures in the newspapers. It wasn't easy, but it was fun.

During summer, the trees in full bloom would fill up my view of the sky with their red and orange, and sometimes, yellow flowers. My aunt told me that the tree was also called the Tree of Fire. I loved collecting the fallen flowers from them, sometimes putting them in my hair and sometimes, making patterns with them on the ground. And when we would take our seat on one of the small stools to get our hands adorned with mehendi, the mehendiwallah would let us sit in this bed of flowers.

Over the years, I developed a fondness for one mehendiwallah in particular: Gupta ji. He talked incessantly, cracking jokes that barely made me laugh as he cackled loudly at every anecdote. Every year, he'd tell me and my sister the same stories and make the same peacock design on our hands. When our aunt fed us sweets from the shop, he'd smile and say, 'There's nothing like spending time with aunts.' Later, our aunt would head for home to prepare dinner, having handed us ₹10 for the return rickshaw fare.

The smell of the mehendi would blend with that of the ghee-laden sweets, creating a charming atmosphere. We, two girls, would bring our hands together to see whose peacock was the prettiest, whose paisley the finest and whose flower the biggest. It was our favourite thing to do.

We'd sit there, patiently, blowing air on our little hands. Every year, Gupta ji gave us the same tips on achieving the brightest colour. 'Don't get the design wet. Put a mixture of lemon juice and sugar on it when you get home. After it's dried, scrape it off with the back of a spoon, then apply a stimulating balm.'

We'd ask him to repeat the formula each year—the proportions of sugar and lemon, the time it would take to dry off and so on.

When it was time to leave, Gupta ji would help us climb into the rickshaw and say the same thing, 'One day, I'll put mehendi on you to the elbows and on the feet—many, many peacocks and paisleys.'

We'd giggle, 'On the feet?'

His eyes would then be moist.

At home, my sister and I would be the princesses, fed dinner till the mehendi was dry and scraped off on a sheet of newspaper in the garden. A bottle of Vicks, with its overpowering smell, would be carefully applied to the designs, which were by then orange. It was my favourite memory of the time I spent both with my aunt and my sister. At sunrise, we'd compare and admire the many shades of cheerful orange. 'Gupta ji is the best,' we'd say.

When the mehendi would begin to fade, I'd start counting the days left for the next summer break (our schools forbid henna'ed hands) when we'd be again allowed to get mehendi on our hands; the wait starting with every goodbye we said to Gupta ji. The ritual lived with us till my sister passed out from school; now she could get her hands henna'ed anytime she wanted, and I felt lonely sitting on that bench, each summer. My sister was now in college, but she remembered our favourite memory. And I knew that for a few summers later, Gupta ji was invited home. It was my sister's wedding and she had said, 'Gupta ji is the best.'

He was in our living room and my sister and I were caught between a gasp and a giggle. She was indecently staring at his hands now—his nails and fingers to be precise. While he kept talking, she kept staring. My mum nudged her, hinting that she was making him uncomfortable. But her eyes were fixed on the flashy orange remnants of mehendi covering his fingertips and nails.

The familiarity and warmth with which he met my aunt, Mum, me and my sister was inexplicable. It was as if the passing years were immaterial. When he walked in, his gait suggested he owned the place and he was here to perform his self-designated role in the wedding. He remarked how excited he was and wished my sister love and happiness. My mum responded with equal ease, borne from years of association and bonding.

Once pleasantries had been exchanged, he started both questioning and answering, unceasingly. My sister just kept nodding, staring at the *orange.* The colour quotient of the mehendi was a big deal during weddings, and my sister knew a lot about it. Orange meant a bright future, and black, a loving mother-in-law. Years of singing and dancing at weddings had familiarised her with the meaning behind the swatches. Orange had no business in the world of bridal mehendi. It had to be black, not only because it looked classier and finer, but also because it was directly proportional to the love you were due to receive from your mother-in-law. Some even suggested that black represented the love you could expect from the husband.

When the date, time and charges were decided, he looked at my sister and said, 'Don't worry, it will be black, the way you want it.' And he left.

The wedding was perfect, the mehendi was black and I heard my sister tell Gupta ji that he indeed was the best. Gupta ji left our home with his eyes damp once again, bidding us goodbye just as he used to do when we were kids. 'I'll come back when it's your turn,' he said to me.

***

Do you want a groom and bride painted on your hands? Or would you prefer a tabla and sitar? Or will it be Saraswati Maa and Durga Maa? And yes, of course, we could inscribe the name of your husband-to-be. Do you want his name in Hindi or English? We could spread the letters of his name over both hands and hide it behind the daisies and paisleys! Do you want the design to go as far as the elbows? Some brides like their arms fully covered.

I'd never faced such a barrage of questions. But I'd heard them all before, in my obsessive mehendi-handed life;

decorated every summer break and every festival from Raksha Bandhan to Diwali. In the busy markets, when the world was going crazy buying juices, wafers and cookie hampers for friends and families, I'd be dragging mostly my aunt, and occasionally Mum or Dad, to Gupta ji, and my hands would be adorned with many, many peacocks.

Today, I was feeling lost. Gupta ji was nowhere to be seen.

We also do Arabic designs. We'd dedicate two people to the bridal mehendi; two more would take care of cousins, aunts and friends. Do you want a package for 50 or do you want to pay per person? Will everyone want it full on both hands? Or would some prefer a 'bale'? Are you allergic to mehendi oil? Also, we don't mix colour in our mehendi, it's natural. We soak it for days and you'd be happy with the results. How many artists do you need in the evening? Four should do fine for the morning mehendi at home . . .

The mehendiwallah was still talking. We were in the same market in front of the sweet shop, trying to finalise a mehandiwallah for my wedding. My eyes were looking for Gupta ji, he'd appear, there'll be a miracle I'd told Mum. He had promised he'd make his second appearance at our home. We had enquired about him, but he had gone missing. No one picked at the number printed on his business card, which now bore a time-worn pale hue, and I was feeling sad. I knew anyone could do the designs, but Gupta ji had a promise to keep.

And then this mehendiwallah took out many bulky albums, placing two on the table and handing over two each to me, my aunt and Mum. Then he called out for my dad and handed him the remainder.

His gaze was making me nervous. But he meant business and was in no mood for random banter, indecent staring, lost memories or silly laughter.

'No, I don't want a picture of the bride and groom.'

(She isn't excited about the wedding.)

'I don't want his name.'

(She doesn't love him enough. And she's not even aware of the post-wedding game where the husband looks for his name in the design on the wife's palms.)

'I don't want the gods and goddesses sketched.'

(She's an atheist.)

'I don't want the modern Arabic designs.'

(She's not 'modern'.)

'Whatever happened to the days when they just drew a simple peacock surrounded by many paisleys?' I'd said the unthinkable. I was missing Gupta ji.

Silence.

The shortlisted mehendiwallah instantly took back all his albums. Excited brides with their hands in the air for a clearer view. Nervous brides with their legs awkwardly splayed on two chairs. Tired brides standing crookedly to flaunt the designs on their hands and legs. And more. All the pictures were safely back in his large black bag.

But he was still smiling.

The client is always right.

It was my turn to return the warmth. 'I love all your designs. All I wanted was a nice design, taking up almost every inch. I don't want you to fill up the tips. And I don't want any checkered patterns. And yes, to the elbows and the knees.' I had simple demands.

We were communicating. He noted the date of my wedding in his book, next to many other dates, many other bride's names. Gupta ji, would have not scribbled the name, he would have remembered. I would have been more than a *client.*

'It'd be exciting to be little girls again. We'd compare and admire the shades next morning,' my sister said, reading my mind.

I was aching for the warmth of the years of association.

I missed the simple peacock that Gupta ji had made for me, for years. Or was it a butterfly?

Had so much time passed?

'One day, I'll put mehendi on you to the elbows and on the feet, many, many peacocks and paisleys.'

***

I didn't know where to start looking for Gupta ji. It never occurred to me that one day he'd be gone. My only contact with him was the spot under the tree, the pew he occupied. I'd never even thought that I'd even need his number to look for him. I'd just find him, smiling and waiting for me with the mehendi cone in his hand. He'd notice me, and just like always, he'd stop everything he was doing and wave at me, his right hand indicating I sit next to him, on the bench. He'd repeat the old jokes, his laughter filling up the air.

Over the years, I'd observed his hair had begun to thin, the grey strands outnumbering the black, and at times, the orange, the latter the result of him rubbing the excessive henna from the cone onto his hair. He was growing old, now surrounded by mehendiwallahs who were half his age. Other than youth, they were equipped with modern business promotion offers, designs and speed. Gupta ji never complained how he didn't have an heir to pass the pew, skill, clientele and traditions. He smiled often.

Where was Gupta ji now? I shuddered at the thought. Was it death or poverty that took him away? Was he breathing his last, lying on a bed, with no children, no family to hold his hand? Was it only him who had a promise to keep? Did I too, not have a promise to keep? What was my self-designated role in his home, his life?

Was I not to honour the scent of henna? Was I not to pay tribute to the man, who'd in every little design prayed for my happiness? Was it not my turn to return the smile? Was I not to respect the colour of the henna?

I looked back.

The brief, quick changes that had become a part of me, unknowingly. My aunt now dyed her hair. A handful of trees on the lane had been chopped. The sweet shop now sold sugar-free, no-ghee options of the treats. The little girls on the benches wore flower hair bands made of shiny silk and satin. The rickshaws were now parked in a corner, and two-wheelers and four-wheelers ruled the roads. Stick-on henna tattoos were on sale too.

Did Gupta ji leave on will? Had we, collectively, hurt his sentiments? Was it us who snatched him off the purity of his profession, the aroma of the leaves?

***

Marigolds on every window pane, the scent of the pacifying flower filling up the room. My little brother as DJ, making last-minute changes to the playlist. Friends unpacking their suitcases, showing one another their outfits and jewellery, seeking approval. Calls from the cook for breakfast going unheard until an uncle takes charge of the situation. My little niece, making mountains of numerous pillows lying on mattresses on the floor, climbing and falling. The sound of the tap running; a happy queue to brush teeth. The help picking up empty coffee and tea mugs from every corner, every room. My mother running around with bags in her hands one moment, boxes the next, then re-appearing with sheets, packets, fruits, clothes, etc. The ironing man collecting *zardozi* sarees, linen shirts and cotton-silk kurtas, carefully listening to each instruction for every piece of cloth.

Our home had never looked this busy, beaming with happiness and activity.

I'm rubbing my eyes with delight and in sleep. Everyone passing by the spot where I'm sitting stops to embrace me. A kiss from a friend, seeing me after many years. A hug from the aunt who took me for my first haircut. A smile from a cook who knows I hate brinjal. A blessing from the uncle who took my mum for her first haircut. A nod from a colleague who'd be filling up my position at work, when I leave. A wink from the senior at college who thought I'd never accept I was in love.

The mehendi team gets to work. Old newspapers are brought out and spread over the rugs and sheets in the living room. Tiny bottles of mehendi oil are neatly arranged on the sheet. Several mehendi cones find places next to them. Low-level benches are brought for the men-in-charge. The stage is set. I change into a pair of old crop pants and a sleeveless t-shirt and sit on the single-seater couch, just like my sister had eight years back. She appears from nowhere and places two cushions at my sides. *Been there, done that.* I feel comfortable now; hands resting on the cushions, feet up. Let's get started.

Just the right amount of oil is applied on the arms, hands, legs and feet and the artists get to work. The designs are exquisite: stems, flowers, curvy lines, peacocks, circles, et al. Everybody looking on, remarking how beautiful they are. The mehendiwallahs look up occasionally, rubbing the dripping mehendi from the cones to their hair.

Soon, little bowls containing a mix of lemon juice and sugar arrive, and just about everyone in the room knows what to do. Using cotton balls, we swab the mixture onto each other's hands. Everyone's mehendi has to look nice and bright; there's no competition or rivalry here.

I see my aunt, standing in the corner smiling, her eyes moist. I am once again the child, standing on the step ladder, knowing she'd not let me fall. She will never stop looking out for me.

***

The mehendi is a success. We dance, sing and don't express our tiredness.

'At night, you can put your hands above a pan with *laung* in it, followed by the stimulating balm; it'll make the mehendi colour darker, black.' And with that, Gupta ji had left. There's absolutely no questioning this nugget of wisdom. My sister had done so, back then, as was suggested by the expert.

It was my turn now. I didn't want any advice from the mehendiwallah and his team at my wedding. I didn't want to be rude or judge their wisdom, but I had observed and heard the words from the *best.*

Everyone is getting ready to sleep. I am in my room. Tomorrow, I will be leaving this home behind.

I look around. I'm the only one with designs up to the elbows and on the feet, up to the knees.

I am the bride.

The smell of henna. I bring my hands closer and take in a deep breath.

It makes me happy, the sharp and familiar smell.

The next morning, my mehendi is black. There are many, many peacocks and a paisley too. Just like Gupta ji would have made.

***

I've never seen a henna tree growing. I am unaware if it grows tall like the gulmohar or not. Does it bear flowers, I know not. What colour are its flowers—orange or white? Are its leaves a light or a dark green? But there's one thing I know. I understand the scent of the tree—a scent that I absorbed in my growing-up years and took with me as I entered a new phase of my life.

*****

A BIGGER PLACE, WITH MORE FEET

I'm a wealthy cobbler. You probably think that's an oxymoron. I can't blame you for that. Like everyone else, you too believe that cobblers are just meant to mend shoes, not set up businesses and get rich. But I'm different; I was born to amass a fortune.

My childhood home was occupied by four brothers, three sisters, a mother, a father, two plates and three mattresses. There was never enough love, space or money, just too many people.

I could have made the force of numbers work in my favour; with a staff of nine (10 including me), I could have set up a business in my small town, but then my father took up drinking day and night, and many things changed. My mother lost the will to live, my brothers began to gamble and follow in our father's footsteps, and my sisters married three village men, who paid for their meals and clothing. Suddenly, I was alone. I left home. I didn't want to decay in poverty. I moved to a bigger town, a metropolis.

I found out how to earn power and sought it out.

I'd never worked for anyone, not even my father, and was certain I didn't want to work for anyone but would be my own master. On my third day in the big town, I announced to the universe that I'd be a rich cobbler.

***

It all began on a March morning. On a bus ride, my right rubber chappal broke; the left strap of the 'V' came away. It didn't disturb me. Poor people don't worry about things breaking—straps, soles, hearts or bones. I rifled through the big, green polythene bag that I always carried with me and took out a spool of thread and a needle. After leaving the bus, I sat under a tree, which also served as a bus-stop. The tree was covered in lovely yellow flowers, many of which had fallen onto the ground. Feeling like a king sitting on the yellow spread, I began to mend my chappal, a simple style with scissor-shaped straps glued to a flat piece.

The process was familiar. My mother had taught all of us the running stitch and we used it often to mend shirt patches or broken chappals. I passed the durable black thread through the eye of the needle, made a knot in the other end, and brought the needle through the rubber till the knot hit the sole. Then, I made stitches to the left and right of the thread entry point, repeating them on the right side, thrice each time. I'd given my chappal a new incarnation, its fifth, having been worn out four times by one of my elder brothers.

I was an expert at mending slippers, something I did for my brothers every now and then, but I began to realise that while their feet were spreading, their gambled assets and brains were shrinking. And that is when I began to think about leaving home to become a cobbler in a bigger place, with more feet.

When I was at home, I never wasted time earning money for education. In our town, many people went to school, yet slept hungry, each night. I saw that time spent in classrooms would never bring me any good, so I began my lessons in life under a tree, where my brothers and father gambled at cards.

Years of poverty had taught me that only the fittest survive. So, while my brothers gambled, I improved my skills: mending chappals, eavesdropping on the lives of others and trying to pocket their winnings. These were vital for my new life as a businessman in the making. I failed at stealing from them. I could never keep a straight face, but I excelled at the mending and eavesdropping. I had a tough time when it came to lying too. I could never hide my true feelings about my father and always ended up hurting Mother. However, what I did learn from observing all the gambling was that lying, stealing and deceiving could be fast ways of making money.

At each game, I hovered around the spot playing with dusty tyres, rolling and running with them. When I was bored with that and had annoyed everyone with my frantic games, I'd sit down and start mending a chappal of one of the players: neighbour, winner, brother, uncle, friend or loser. They'd let me sit by their side and stitch, cut, fold, re-cut, nail and stick.

Ecstatic in victory or gloomy in defeat, the players would slip into any pair of chappals I placed next to them. They never appreciated my quick work or noticed the change of style from scissor-shaped straps to broad, horizontal ones with buckles. They never paid me for my repair work or realised how my slippers lasted much longer than the ones they'd previously worn. They never remarked at the black tyre resulting in a brown slipper or how the heels I added made them look taller. They never wondered how my slippers fitted them perfectly without me measuring their feet or noticed I was now making new slippers and sandals, rather than merely mending the ones they wore. They never questioned why I worked tirelessly or left one day for the big town.

Reckoning that you can't play with broken shoes, I set up the first of my cobbler shops in the big town outside an amusement park, under a tree next to the ticket window. As my first step towards becoming a businessman, I nailed a woollen thread on the trunk and hung shoe soles from it: black, brown and grey. I made myself comfortable on a tyre I'd brought from home, and laid out my tools on an upside-down cola crate picked up from the garbage dump outside the park. My tools of the trade were scissors, hammer, adhesive, pencil, knife, wax and brass nails.

I didn't have much in the way of resources, but I had many hours and plenty of broken shoes to mend.

The pink-coloured sandals worn by little girls made squeaky sounds.

The blue-coloured shoes worn by little boys lit up.

The superheroes and princesses were the favourites.

Velcro was a modern adhesive.

Straps, buckles and laces were for bigger kids.

Children: Noted.

Colours, graphics, sounds and lights: Noted.

Parents never say no to children: Lesson.

In six months, I learnt how young feet changed, quickly and suddenly, between their first and second visits to the park. I took note of ages, heights and sizes. I learnt that girls loved heels, but their mums didn't allow them to wear those. I learnt that the boys broke their shoes faster than the girls.

I learnt that any shoe that pinched or caused discomfort was discarded within minutes.

My next stop was another yellow flower-bearing tree outside a girls' college. I was 24 and the sight of girls made me work harder and kept me happier. My day began early; seven in the morning. The girls would rush up to me, slipper in hand, for repair before attending their first class. There was always a broken shoe here: a cracked strap, a wobbly heel, a dangling buckle, a loose sequin or a falling flower. The reasons behind the damage were numerous: an inexpensive fashion purchase, a crowded bus, a missed step, a hurried walk or a sudden change of plan, leaving no time to return home and change. There'd be an urgent requirement for shoes that matched an outfit, needing them to be fixed immediately.

My tools now included a stitching awl, pincers, threads of various colours, more needles, half-moon and half-circle knives and a shoe stand.

I loved it when the girls limped towards me, waiting to be rescued. I was their knight in shining armour. With just one stitch, I'd bring smiles to their faces. I'd smile back and we'd talk. They'd tell me where they'd bought their last pairs of shoes and how much they'd paid for them.

I'd hear them discuss how heels hurt their feet if they walked too long or stood for hours. I noticed their mums sharing their shoes with them. I observed how women could wear it all: sandals, shoes, slippers, heels, platforms and *juttis*. I understood that nothing else really mattered, except how a pair looked on them.

The chappals are worn by a girl in a kurta with pants or salwar-kameez.

The two-inch heels are worn by a girl in a skirt.

The sturdy sports shoes are worn by a girl in a pair of running shorts or track pants.

The delicate lace ballerinas are worn by a girl in a dress.

Anything worked with a pair of denims.

Women: Noted.

Colours, styles, heels and designs: Noted.

Women always need more than a dozen pairs of shoes: Lesson.

It was outside the college that I found out all about colours (purple looks best with green, yellow is a summer colour, and black is a must-have), love (each day, I gave a yellow flower from the tree to a different girl) and a future worker for my empire-to-be.

Next to my cobbler's den stood Prakash, an ice cream seller. He envied me for many reasons. During summer, his earnings were decent, but in winter he earned very little. I, on the other hand, earned throughout the year. Throughout all the seasons, I charged just ₹1 or ₹2 or ₹5 for my repair work, while he charged ₹10. But at the end of the day, I made more money than him. The girls offered to buy me ice cream sometimes, standing next to me and chatting while I mended their footwear. When I was sick and off work, they felt my absence, asking Prakash what had happened to me.

We only competed for the affection of girls, not in business. The girls never truly loved any of us; the boys they liked asked me if I could polish their shoes for ₹1. I'd refuse, telling them I was a cobbler, not a polish boy.

Prakash didn't like me and I didn't like him much either, but he had one thing I admired—the ability to steal, lie and cheat with a straight face.

A few months of my setting up shop here, a college girl told me she'd seen Prakash stealing money from under the mat I sat on. Every time he sat next to me and we shared his lunch, he sidled away with a few coins. I knew how to count, but I wasn't sure how best to catch a thief.

I let him do so for another month, aware that he had a wife and son to look after. I had no family.

I'd tried my hand at stealing in my town, the red of my face, giving it away, each time. Prakash was different; he would not bat an eyelid, his face would not change colour and his hands would not tremble.

At lunchtime, I began to notice how his hands moved in between washing his hands, folding a roti, gulping down a bowl of dal, and nicking coins and notes. I began to enjoy this game; my failure of being unable to catch him in the act. To test him, I manufactured challenges: changing the spot where I kept money every few days—under the mat, in the tool box, inside a shoe, or at times, sending him an open invitation to perform by humbly requesting him to guard my shop while I went to the bathroom. Each time, I lost, for the folds of the mat were intact and the shoes bore an untouched look.

Each night, I began to look forward to counting how much Prakash had pocketed from me, under my now 'watchful' eyes. His deftness was comparable to that of a magician. I began to wonder if it was a gift he was born with. Poverty does impart one with skills that the rich find hard to imagine or find pleasure scowling at.

A smart thief, however, he had no control over his urge to steal—not knowing when to stop or pause, and believing that the subject at the receiving end was blindfolded at all times. His talent and my inability to catch formed the blueprint of my plan. Would he cheat from me? As a boss, it worried me, but then a businessman has to take certain risks and be prepared for a few losses, and at times, also let his employees believe that they are the real bosses.

I didn't get impatient to bring him on board; it had to wait till I finished my 'education'. It was now time for me to move to my third spot, under a tree that was outside an office building.

The buildings were tall, obscuring the skies. Most men here wanted their shoes polished: I was at a loss. Others wanted their shoe laces changed. I added laces to my tools, along with rubber, plastic, polyurethane and leather soles. A few of the men just wanted blobs of adhesive to keep their soles in place. They all wore the same shoes, in similar colours. I noticed they were comfortable with slip-ons, but mostly wore shoes with buckles or laces. On Fridays, they wore sandals with buckles and shoes in colours other than black and brown. I was surprised to see the women working with them and their shoes began to interest me—block, pencil and kitten heels; strappy, lacy and string sandals; ankle, rain and high boots.

Leather was a favourite. No one shied away from buying and flaunting expensive shoes.

Shoes should always be shiny, never dirty.

Noisy heels were only for women; men's shoes should be silent.

The same pair could be worn throughout the week.

Men: Noted.

Formal, informal, fabric and cost: Noted.

Men noticed the shoes worn by both genders. Women couldn't distinguish between men's shoes, mostly: Lesson.

I also noticed these men and women were always busy, either leaving meetings or heading to others. They never had time to talk to me. Five months later, my learning was over. I decided to move. It was now time to work on my business plan.

But it had to wait.

The next morning, I received a letter from my eldest sister informing me that our mother had passed away the week before.

I wasn't asked to return home. Mother's last rites had been performed in my absence. My sister was expecting her third child and asked me to be a good uncle and send money for the child.

I cried that night; they were my first and last moments of despair. I missed my mother, reminded of the times how she was before Father began to drink. I cursed my father, wondering if he'd even noticed she'd gone. That night, I made a pair of beautiful shoes in yellow and gold. I imagined my mother wearing them and looking happy.

I don't know when winter gave way to summer; it must have been somewhere between my sister's 'begging' letter and me moving to a new place at the vegetable market. I shed tears here as I made shoes through the long nights, grieving at the loss of my mother and the hopelessness of ever having a family fuelling my ambition.

At the vegetable market, the vendors spoke my language. I found comfort in their words. I cried in front of them. I felt easy talking to them. They made meals for me, they let me grieve. They said prayers for my mother, for her peace. I made shoes for them. Black shoes for children, sandals and heels for the women, slippers and loafers for the men, and cushioned chappals for the elderly. I didn't quote prices for the shoes, and took whatever they gave me: money, food, sympathy, alcohol, blessings, suggestions and requests.

On my last day at the market, I sent a letter to my sister saying I'd spent the money meant for my unborn nephew or niece. She never wrote to me again. I didn't expect or wait for her to write to me, either. The same evening, I went to visit Prakash with my proposal.

He was surprised to see me, but welcomed me into his home. His son, 14, now sold ice cream, while Prakash polished shoes at a boys' college. He was smart, I told him so. When his wife and son left us alone to talk and eat dinner, I asked him if he liked being surrounded by the boys. He said he didn't. Next, I told him I wanted him to steal for me. He looked shocked.

I told him, 'You have to return what you took from me.'

He didn't ask for forgiveness, nor did his eyes show any sign of fear or guilt. He was the right candidate. It would have been foolish of me to tell him that it was not me, but the college girls who caught him first, so I stayed quiet about that. He offered no excuse either. 'When do I start?' he asked.

I trained him for two months to identify a useless shoe from a useful shoe. A broken sole, but a perfect strap would work. Common shoe sizes were the best picks. Some shoes could be repaired, some re-made. Fabric could be cut, dyed and patched. Buttons, straps, buckles, laces and adornments never went to waste. Never pick just a single shoe, always a pair.

On the last day of his training, I showed him the spots he'd be stealing shoes from—outside five temples. Devotion to the gods drew masses, who as a mark of respect worshipped the idols, barefoot, their shoes left unattended outside the places of worship. He knew how to steal. He was needy. I was ambitious, trained, smart and inventive.

The plan was clear—working out the worship rush hours to maximise our opportunities. Our timetable followed the prayer schedule: Mondays for Lord Shiva, Tuesdays for Lord Hanuman, Wednesdays off, Thursdays for Lord Vishnu, Fridays for goddesses Lakshmi, Durga Maa and Santoshi Maa, Saturdays for fighting the influence of the planet Mars and Sundays for those who hadn't had time to pray on weekdays. The festive season saw long queues, with rich and poor praying at different locations. The police vans patrolled just once a week and the people always had something to ask their gods for. Dull days were a rarity. Prakash worked by day, I worked at night. I never saw him at his job, and he never saw me at mine.

Every evening, he delivered the loot on time, sans fear or guilt. I knew this association would last. I encouraged him to train his son too and he agreed. He gave up polishing shoes completely. I gave him enough to keep him content and quiet.

Every night, I picked the useless from the useful, making two piles. A sole from here, a heel from there, a strap from one, a buckle from another, a flower from a woman's shoe, an umbrella from a child's shoe, a pin from a dying shoe, a tongue from a living one, a left welt, a right waist and lace holes from the remnants.

After every three months, I asked Prakash to take a break.

As he relaxed, I took a bus to the nearest small or big town, to sell my creations. The men loved the class. The women loved the style. The children loved the colours. My collection of shoes stood out; no shoe looked like another or the original. I too, looked different. I dressed up as a merchant.

When I was done, I'd return to work. Before anyone could notice Prakash or the missing slippers, we would have shifted to another part of town, another temple. There are believers everywhere.

I worked hard and lived well. I was a happy man. I realised fostering relationships was pointless.

And in between selling at town bazaars and local shoe shops, learning about new materials and techniques, observing people and fashions, planning well and executing better, I became a rich city cobbler at 26.

I never invested in a permanent home, any kind of attachment was pointless—with an item or an individual. Prakash never asked me what I did with the steal. I believed he knew it though, but I was confident he would never attempt to replicate. He lacked both my skill and drive.

Over the next one year, I introduced no changes to our work plan. He stole, I created. I advised him to keep a low profile, he followed. I too never wore a shoe or a smirk that would give away my secret. In our homes, we slept and ate better. I owned four mattresses now, though I used only one. I looked at the extra items, spelling my success.

But in business, one has to taste failure and I was prepared for it: the day when Prakash would make a mistake. He didn't know when to pause. I was asleep when it happened, with a night's work ahead.

In the evening, when Prakash didn't show up with the shoes, I went to his home. His son told me his father had been arrested. I asked the boy his name, and he said Deepak. I gave Deepak some money to free his father from the jail and also to stay quiet. I was not curious to know how he got caught. I took care of him, making lying easier and lucrative for him. When free, he would have enough money to eat both a sabji and dal for the next one year, thrice a day. I also knew he would be freed in no time. When the men in uniform would have their fill of beating him up, they'd let him go. The number of poor who stole or cheated outnumbered the space per square metre in the jail. There was never enough space, just too many people, it reminded me of my once home.

I felt the loss of my employee, but I had learnt everything was replaceable in a town, in a business.

As I left Prakash's home, I asked, 'Deepak, are you coming along with me?'

The very next day, his son and I moved to another, far bigger town.

***

I always sat under a tree that bore yellow flowers. I never bothered to know by what name the tree was called. My mother wore yellow flowers in her hair. When Father began to drink, she stopped wearing them. The golden slippers I made for Mother, now lie in a corner of my home, gathering dust. Fostering relationships with the dead or the alive is pointless.

*****

OVER A CUP OF CHAI

A tiny, lazy town; it had always been so, but this town was draped in colours. It was home to many green trees and that made up for everything else that it lacked. The trees, in turn, were home to many colourful birds. Many labelled the town as *dead*—perhaps they couldn't hear the chirping of the birds that brought the town *alive* with each sunrise. Countless amaltas trees bloomed here and their yellow flowers carpeted the concrete roads. Amidst these was one tall fellow, soaring high on the university grounds of the town. And under its umbrella, generations indulged in cups of simple, humble, milky-brown chai.

SONIA

I miss walking under the shade of a row of amaltas trees that lined up my pathway to the university—the path strewn with yellow flowers that created a shimmering trail. When Rhea was a child, I would often take her to the university with me, secretly nurturing a dream to watch my little girl walk on the same path. We'd walk up to it, irrespective of wherever in the town we were heading to or from, it was a small town. 'The grounds are the largest thing in the whole town,' she'd say when we'd reach the playing field that was nestled between many short and tall buildings serving as departments and hostels for students pursuing post-graduation in various subjects.

She and I spent many winter mornings there. She'd run and skip in the grounds, while I sat and drank tea from a glass tumbler. 'The warmest university ritual,' I'd tell her, pointing to Sharma aunty's tea stall. It wasn't really a stall, just a spot under a tall tree. The spot was occupied by a huge steel vessel, a kerosene pump action stove, a dozen glass tumblers and a large glass jar filled with rusks, all jostling for space on the newspaper sheets underneath. Mostly, I'd sit on one of the three rocks facing the stall. At other times, I made myself comfortable on the pavement to the left of it. The stall was as noisy as it was when I lived in the campus. 'It feels like I never left,' I would tell Aunty, on each visit, over each cup of tea. She would nod in agreement, sitting just the way she always had with her legs folded on a scruffy gunny bag.

Later, I'd walk Rhea to the Department of English and Cultural Studies, the place where I once studied Aristotle and Shakespeare. It would be hard to contain the excitement in my voice as we stepped inside the doors. I'd point to the notice board, 'Nothing has changed. They still put on acts of *Saint Joan*.' By then, Rhea too knew that *Saint Joan* was George Bernard Shaw's most memorable play and my favourite too. I'd greet the peon and mention I was an ex-student and wanted to show my daughter around. 'Quietly,' he'd say, 'The lectures are on.' Once permitted, I'd peek inside the classrooms, library and auditorium, using Rhea as an 'excuse'. Minutes later, I'd walk out with a big smile on my face, being the university girl once again.

The 'then' and 'now' game was exciting, even decades later after having passed out from the department. In 1981, three years after I left the campus, I'd married and moved to a bigger town, but I kept returning to the stall. As Rhea grew up, she got busier with her studies and it became difficult for her to accompany me. So, I began to drop by for a cup sometimes alone, and many times with my husband. I am not sure if he enjoyed the tea as much as I did, but he gave me company nevertheless.

Rhea would often ask, 'What's so special about the tea?' Her curiosity regarding this ritual was genuine, but I found it hard to come with a suitable explanatory answer. I only hoped she'd get to taste it herself and find her own answers in the many tumblers she'd consume.

It was not a tradition, but I wished she could study at my alma mater. And so when her entrance results came through and it was time to pack and leave, I was beaming with pride. But this time around, I was moist eyed as we walked into the doors of the department and it was Rhea who held my hand and walked me in, stopping by at the notice board, helping me relax, 'Nothing has changed.' My little girl had grown up.

'It feels like home, Mum,' Rhea said, as she walked into the hostel gates. After we said our goodbyes, my husband and I shared a cup of tea. From a distance, I saw Aunty; she looked fatigued and older too. No one knew how old she was; just that she'd served tea to generations of many families and the very thought put me at ease. I noticed the glass tumblers were gone, replaced with styrofoam cups. The tea now cost ₹2, it was 25 paisa in my days. Aunty was at work, following the same routine, working each day from 7:00 am to 7:00 pm. 'Nothing had changed.'

RHEA

It was hard to imagine Sharma aunty as a young woman; she was old from the very first time I saw her—grey hair, watery eyes and a weathered face. She always wore a faded threadbare saree, tied in a hurry; it had more wrinkles than her face. When she would notice Mum walking towards the stall, she'd call out to her helper, a 10-year-old boy, 'Ek pheeki chai for Sonia.' The boy, dressed in a pair of khaki shorts with a clean white vest, would know a VIP guest had arrived and would hurry up in serving. Mum would smile and Aunty would smile back, her milky eyes sparkling. 'How does she know your name?' I'd ask Mum, and Aunty would reply, 'I even know her class roll number.' And they'd both laugh, heartily.

During my first week on the campus, I walked up to Aunty's tea stall. And while seven years is a plenty of time for the changing and forgetting of faces to happen, Aunty recognised me instantly, 'Sonia's big girl.'

I was embarrassed at first, but then I did what I'd seen Mum do over the years. I hugged her and asked if she was keeping well. I told her how school and college had kept me busy and she said she understood. She looked older than I could have imagined. Her voice was feeble, hair winter-white, and the crows' feet at her eyes had deepened. She poured a serving for me in a styrofoam cup—her hands were shaking and her fingers crooked. The young boy, her helper, was now wearing full pants and a bushirt. He carried more than a dozen tea cups on a small tray with notches holding each.

This was the first time I tasted her tea; more water, less milk and lots of sugar, as she'd been making it for 43 years now. It was a diluted version of the tea Mum made at home, and the sweetest thing I'd ever tasted. Truth be told, I didn't like it in the first sip nor even in the first few cups, yet over the following weeks, I'd turned into tea addict.

By my second term, I couldn't keep my eyes open during the morning class without Aunty's concoction, and I wasn't the only one *effected.* Within 15 minutes of the clock striking 8:00 am, Aunty prepared more than 75 cups for the drowsy students. The shop was at its noisiest then, each one of us making urgent demands for the kam doodh-wali chai. We all wanted to survive the first lecture. Vessels would be refilled thrice before the clock struck nine, bringing the university alive. She'd set about her routine of cleaning the vessel, boiling water, adding milk, stirring sugar, pouring cups and giving orders to the helper, while we'd set about ours: bunking classes, making notes, preparing for plays, crafting props and debating endlessly.

During my fourth term in the university, a 24-hour library hall was built facing the tea stall. It was no surprise that we began to drink more tea that year, as the shop remained open till 2:00 am. Aunty was wise enough to hire two more helpers and add five more jars to the space, which now stored vanilla cream biscuits, atta cookies, coconut bites, peanuts and a very salty *namkeen.* The good ol' rusks took up the biggest jar and remained the hottest-selling item on the minimal menu. At seven in the evening, Aunty would hand over the running of the shop to the boys. I can't be sure, but I heard that the boys sold cigarettes after Aunty left. I'll refrain from telling you how many hours we spent outside the library and how many inside, but yes, we managed to befriend the guard and were now allowed to take our tea cups inside. In the best winters I spent on campus, Aunty made us ginger tea in the mornings to treat our sore throats, and in the evenings, we peeled away at egg shells. Hiding behind scarves and cardigans, we scribbled our names and roll numbers on the rocks we sat on. The pavement too became dear to us; it was forgiving for we often spilled our tea on it and covered it with crumbs from rusks and biscuits.

I visited the shop thrice daily: before the first class, at four in the evening before heading back to the hostel, and then at night when I visited the library. Each time, Aunty never failed to smile or participate in our discussions; she knew our teachers, timetables and gangs. At times, she'd join us in imitating our lecturer who taught us the techniques of modern poetry. Over the years, she'd heard many batches imitate him and had begun to empathise with us, especially when he asked us to stay back for extra classes. Although, on a few occasions, she was happy to be a silent observer—holding the tea strainer in her shaky hands and filtering the tea as well as our banter. She knew many girls held onto their cups long after the tea was drained and that the boys obligingly hung around too. She knew that on an average day at least 20 students lost their biscuits while dunking them. The complaints over a biscuit steeped longer than it should have been, and the struggle to remove the resultant soggy shreds would be met with advice on the art of dipping—the optimal holding time. I'd sit there blowing the *malai* off the top of my cup and blaming myself for not drinking the tea when it was hot. I was now living the tea ritual that Mum once lived, sometimes sipping a cup between people I knew and sometimes between people that Aunty knew.

And over many cups, I realised that the stall was a favourite hangout for many ex-students, not just my mum. They'd drop by alone sometimes, and sometimes in a bunch. The ones who stayed in town remained loyal to the tea and often returned between afternoon meetings or on late-night drives. There'd be a few children in the playground too, hopscotching and skipping, while their parents indulged in nostalgia. Not a single individual looked alone in this sea of familiar faces, and cups of tea kept everyone warm. Sometimes, ex-students would decide to have a get-together for old times' sake. Soon, letters, phone calls and emails would begin to chase memories and a reunion would be announced, overjoying Aunty. With every poster plastered on the tree trunk, she began to tell tales of the boys and girls in the batch till the date on the poster arrived. She'd recite their nicknames, first names and surnames, telling us who owned the first bike, and who was the brat. We'd laugh and tell her she could do the roll call when they arrived, and spill the beans too. 'Absolutely,' she'd say.

She spoke with each of us with the same interest, asking us whether we were eating and studying well, looking after us as if we were one of her children. She never married and I never saw anyone visit her either.

'Do you have any family?' I asked her once.

'A huge one,' she said, as she pointed to the scattered groups of students around the stall.

I understood it was a silly question to ask. The routine was as much as hers as ours. We loved her lousy tea and she loved the lousy us. And I had begun to understand why Mum never stopped visiting her and why Aunty remembered Mum's name. For we were not simply drinking tea, we were making memories, and as Mum would say, 'Memories don't have to be perfect; they can be made over imperfect cups of sugary tea with less milk.'

The day of leaving campus arrived sooner than anyone of us would have wanted or imagined. The last week was the toughest to live through. We were exhausted; the exams had been painful, but we all knew that packing up our stuff in the hostel rooms would bring us far more pain. There were no more classes to attend, nor any dull lectures to stay awake through, yet we found ourselves back at the tea stall on each of the last seven days.

The sounds were familiar: the bubbling of water, the stirring of sugar, the opening of jars, the crunching of rusks, the pumping of the stove and the crushing of cups. It was all as per usual. Aunty had consumed her first cup of tea and the drowsy campus was livening with many cups being hurriedly poured. The stove was not tired, promising many more batches and perhaps generations, reflecting the thoughts in Aunty's mind. Amidst the commotion, I sat looking at the boys and girls I had spent the two years of my university life with.

There was the boy everyone misunderstood. The girl who'd dated seniors, juniors and batch mates. The lover, nursing a broken heart. The girl fit for the title of Miss Congeniality. The girl who spoke little and used her left hand whenever she did. The topper everyone disliked. The human calendar who never forgot a birthday. The two boys who fought over an assignment (or was it, as the gossips said, a girl?). The couple getting married next month. The best actor in the class. And me, finding it so hard to say goodbye to the batch of 2003.

Empty glasses were dumped in the bin as fresh ones were poured. Someone made a slurping sound, drinking tea from a plate. Another asked for an extra glass to hold the hot cup. Trickled tea was being wiped off from the floor and cream was being licked off biscuits. And in between all this sharing of gossip, confessing of secrets, fretting over results, exchanging of numbers and worrying over the future, goodbyes were being said.

I don't know who began the leaving and who had the last cup of tea; maybe it was the boy with the loudest voice or the girl who'd made us cry with her farewell speech. Everyone hugged each other and Aunty; a few touched her feet. She blessed one and all, bidding farewell, 'Be good and come back soon.'

It was tricky to guess who'd return and trickier to guess whether Aunty would be around to greet them. But if she were, she'd serve us the special tea and call us by our name, no matter how much we'd changed. I knew she'd be the one most curious to know who RSVP'd for the reunion of this batch of 30 boys and girls.

'So, are you all here?' she'd ask.

'No, there are some absentees,' someone would reply.

Would we all go back soon? I closed my eyes and imagined us sitting on the rocks, after a few years, getting annoyed at being yelled at and called by a nickname we were given in class, laughing out loud at the ridiculous dreams we'd had, mocking the one who was caught cheating in class, shaking hands with the classmate we hoped we'd never see again, flaunting our successes and covering up our mistakes, making excuses for failing to return calls, asking ourselves if it was finally time to forget and forgive and move on, and warming our hands with the tea we'd once consumed as one.

As I drank my last cup of tea, I felt a lump in my throat. The tea was imperfect, the memories around it perfect. With moist eyes, I touched Aunty's feet and hugged her tight, 'I'll look forward to the day when you'll say "tea on the house" for the batch of 2003.'

And just like that I graduated from my mum's university.

Would I return for the tea, like she did?

Yes, because it's rare that life gives you chances to rewind.

SHARMA AUNTY

It was pretty much in the same 'old times' sake' way that the reunion for the batch of 1998 was announced. An ex-student sipped his cup of tea and said, 'It's been so long!' And two months later, the university grounds came alive with nuggets from the past. I saw the chairman and the three lecturers seated on chairs that had been brought from the auditorium. The peon, sweeper and department receptionist were in attendance too.

A handful of students, unaware that their fourth lecturer had passed away, described what a wonderful man and teacher he'd been. 'I can't believe we lost touch,' someone said.

Sitting at my stall on the gunny bag, I thought to myself, 'They've not changed at all, except that they're now better dressed. Look at those ironed clothes and polished shoes.' I'd seen them grow from boys and girls to men and women. My eyes dampened when the batch sat down for a group photograph. 'Who'd have thought they'd grow up so fast!' A few minutes later when they advanced towards the stall, I announced to the helper boys, 'Tea on the house for the batch of 1998.' And just like that it felt that they'd never left.

The first three cups went to three alumni—two boys, one girl—who used to sit on the same bench. Roll No.12 was now a lecturer himself. He showed a picture of his wife and seven-year-old daughter to everyone. The tea was brewing and I was being generous with the milk. The current batches in the university often joked about how I saved the milk for my ex-students, and they were right. 'Maybe when we graduate, you'll add extra milk to our tea too.'

'Oh, how I've longed for this tea!' said the lecturer.

'In my office, they serve only croissants and coffee, no rusks or tea,' said the other man, who'd lost his wife in an accident two years ago. Nobody from the batch had attended the funeral; they'd sent flowers and written notes, but hadn't shown up. Silence fell; the guilt of avoidance was visible in everyone's eyes. Thankfully, he ended the unease; laughter rang out as he said, 'My wife made better tea than you.'

'Does your husband know how to make tea?' they then teased the woman.

A little while later, they began to leave, to get back to their lives, making promises to return soon.

By evening, the stall was back in business and the tea was brewing; turning from lighter hues to darker shades. The sweepers were clearing the ground of reunion remnants; the chairs too were back where they belonged. As for me, I continued to relive the moments, 'That girl you met today is a RJ; the one you hear every day on the radio.' The radio at the stall was blaring loud, another old item in the shop, one that only my students could make work. They'd hit it on the back several times until it began to sing again. 'Ask her to gift you a new radio,' someone laughed as the radio stopped again. And just like that another day came to an end.

With each passing day, I witnessed terms moving closer to its end, and the farewells began to become a part of me.

Until date, the students stay amused with how I remember the Who's Who of the class. I also know they laugh at my bulky green register, one that holds a record of who'd left the campus without clearing their dues. Majority of the students buy tea on credit and I have to keep a tally of the actual number of cups consumed vs. paid for. Yet, I never ask anyone to pay and they don't forget either. However, there are always a few defaulters. From the batch of 1995, five students owe me ₹3 each. I can spot the face, but when they show up, I never remind them of their dues—instead I offer free cups, 'For old times' sake.'

Last week while I was about to retire for the day, I heard a request from a familiar voice. 'Can I paste this poster here on the tree?' asked a tall, beautiful middle-aged woman with long black hair and a dark complexion. The poster read: 'Reunion for the batch of 1990 on 19 November 2014, University Grounds, 11:00 am.' When she was done pasting it, she asked for a special tea. The special tea meant extra milk, an extra spoonful of loose tea and an extra rupee too. 'You look as beautiful as you did back then,' I told her. She handed over her the ₹3 for the tea and I returned it for old times' sake. She touched my craggy feet before she left. Now, I was curious to know if this reunion was just for students or families too. I wondered if she married one of the boys from her batch; five of them in the class proposed to her! I secretly hope that she married Roll No.25. I was particularly fond of this boy. He wasn't pretty, not one of those you take home and cuddle with, but he had a genuine smile and bright eyes.

Roll No. 25 reminded me of another boy, Roll No. 16 from the batch of 1992. He was a regular at the stall, now a man with a paunch. 'He was the fairest, shortest and brightest in the batch. He was rank one in the entrance exam. The lecturer had introduced him like that on the first day of the class.' I told one and all, 'He works in the share market and drives a big car.' I was partial to him; everyone knew that because each time he arrived, one could smell *elaichi* in the air. He'd park his car in the parking lot in front of the library and it drew a lot of attention—perhaps triggered dreams too. He never arrived with a friend. He'd either be on the phone or smoking a cigarette. I'd look at him and wonder why he returned, and hoped he found what he was searching for in the glasses he consumed.

Often, the students tell me that I look weary and they look after me when I look unwell. On days that I am not active and alert to the process of tea preparation or their conversation, they ask me to take a day off. But, neither am I old nor I am tired enough to say goodbye to my large family. So I stay here, for I have promises to keep. I have to look after the children of the ex-students and I have to watch the former leave and then return. And I have to be able to recognise them, even with my failing sight. Maybe they would have changed with time, but my eyes would refute that, for in my tea lies a reflection of their past.

*****

THE FIRST KISS

I'd never kissed under the cover of a dark night in a narrow city lane. It was dirty, known for its naked wires, uncovered manholes and unscrupulous acts. We were standing under the dense branch blanket of a pudgy, bounty tree. The crickets were chirping, rubbing their front wings across ridged back ones. The lilt reached my skin, making me shiver. Were the males sending out courting signals, chirping as they sensed a female around? Intense songs for a quiet winter night. A family of sparrows was sleeping in the tree trunk cavity, peacefully huddled. I watched the grey clouds through the net of branches, waiting impatiently. The leaves swayed slowly, without disturbing the stillness of the hour.

Then we kissed, under the tree in a narrow lane.

All my memories of that night are vivid. I felt unconfined, unconstrained. Standing there in the miasma of rickety buildings and damp love, I tasted passion for the first time. It was bitter, stark, powerful and overwhelming. It was dark and pure, just like the night. I was happy. I was spontaneous. Isn't that what passion is meant to be like?

We kissed once, once more, once again, then stopped. We didn't fear the night guard with his blinding flashlight. We weren't worried about being found. No one watched the bulky tree in the dirty lane, and its smutty secrets were buried with the night. The ailing dogs slumbered under parked cars close by, and a black cat with yellow eyes that shone purred at us. We stopped because this was how far we could have gone.

I looked at him as though it was the first time that I was. A year older and two inches taller, looking older today with his baby face hidden under the few days of facial hair growth. His beard not sculpted with precision, his nails trimmed and clean. The scent of his aftershave reaching me, lingering on. A smooth forehead, with no wrinkles. It was hard to spot signs of daily neglect on his face, in his eyes. He was not smiling, yet his eyes were communicating content.

As I continued to gaze, I felt the tension in my shoulders release. We held hands and sat; the cat stretched out. The metal bars of the bench were cold, its silver paint peeling and left arm-rest broken, a sharp end protruding. The area was strewn with sticks, bird droppings and dew drops. I could feel the chill around me and the filth below. We stayed still, not touching each other. In our hearts, we knew this was it—the beginning and the end. Should we walk back to our homes, where our families waited for us? Or stay a bit longer?

The road ahead was damp, a layer of mist covering it. I was just a few steps away from the home where I belonged. I looked at the pale, shaky building in front of me, and watched the flickering street-light play hide and seek against the black I was wearing. I strained my ears to listen to the sounds from the houses around me: a couple arguing, a child giggling, a television blaring, a pan simmering, a paper rustling. I felt the sweat in my hands; we'd been holding hands for a while.

And then he began to hum a song, an old classic Hindi film number. The moon light filtered through the branches; it sat with us. The melody was gentle. I felt alive. We stood. I closed my eyes and we danced the only dance I knew. His hand was on my waist and my head on his shoulder. I loved the rhythm and mood. It reminded me of my childhood when keeping secrets was fun and forgivable. I'd twirl, falling back into his arms, and he'd hold me tight. I heard the stars applaud our performance. I felt his warmth, the comfort I'd longed for. I don't know how long I swayed, but I know he didn't stop singing till I halted. I opened my eyes. I'd shared my dream with him. It wasn't just mine now—it was ours. It made my heart flutter; if it wanted to beat loud enough for all to hear, I'd let it.

'You think the sparrows will wake up?' I laughed, and he laughed along. Sharing the dream with him made it real. I took a deep breath, soaking in his smell, knowing it will stay with me.

Two was easy; two could share a dream, make a promise and keep a secret.

It was indeed an odd, insane night. I'd let go the inhibitions, crossed the limits and forgotten the rules. And all this for what I knew was not love. It was a whiff of freshness, a wave of freedom. It was a night that didn't feel wrong, a night when I had a lot to say, but chose not to.

'There's no need to make memories,' he said.

So we just sat, half-hugging, half-smiling. But my heart began to wander. I panicked, thinking about the moment when he'd leave my hand and walk across the road. The thud I'd feel when the romance ends. I asked him how long we had.

'Till the crickets stop chirping.'

I let their shrill songs give me goose bumps until the last moment. I surveyed the sparrows; I'd never seen them sleep before. Hidden in the cavity, they felt safe. I longed to sleep like that.

A shoulder was offered for me to rest on. As I shut my eyes, I wondered what the eyes of my family and friends would say to me. They'd judge me if they could read through me. May be they'd pounce on me. I'd done the unthinkable. But I'd tell them no one had seen us and perhaps that would put them at ease. 'We were on the bench under that pudgy tree.'

I slept well for a while till he woke me up, whispering, 'It's time to go.'

I picked up a dead flower and he put it in my hair.

I let him go first.

As I walked back home, I hoped and wailed. I was angry and helpless. 'It's the poetry of abandonment,' I told myself. 'Something noble.'

I stepped out of my black pants and into my pyjamas. I went to bed, next to my wife.

'It wasn't just a kiss, it was my right,' I told myself.

It was the first time I'd kissed a man.

*****

ON THE BED OF WOOD

When imagining tricky scenarios, I used to visualise banana peels, muddy puddles and food poisoning just before a poetry recital at school. As I grew older and had more to lose, I thought about tough moments often—even when I was in labour and driving myself to the hospital (my husband travels a lot for work), I worried about the house being robbed and losing my job. Then there was that time Mum called in the middle of the night saying she couldn't wake Dad up. It made me shiver and I immediately feared the worst. Like anyone else, I dreaded failure, falls, loneliness and loss, with thoughts of disease terrifying me the most. But even though the little voice in my head sometimes sounded off about sudden death, I wasn't prepared for that day.

I hoped I'd live long enough to fret over grey hair and missed medications, or at least tick off the few things I'd planned to do before I turned 32—trekking with my husband, knitting a sweater for my son, cutting my hair really short, mastering Thai cuisine, going on a holiday with my girlfriends (the 'mommy' gang) and becoming the senior manager at my firm.

Yes, I'd thought about dying too, but I'd never imagined myself lying on a funeral pyre.

I'd seen myself covered in blood, struggling to breathe, and even heard the doctors tell my husband they'd done everything they could for me. But when they placed me on the bed of wood, I realised it *really* was time to say goodbye. All the preparations—will making, insurance, powers of attorney—never equip you for the bed of wood or to watch your loved ones cry helplessly.

I was laid out on stacked layers of short, round pieces of wood—balanced, stable. Under the three-feet-high bed was a metal grate. I was short, merely five feet and an inch; not much room was required to accommodate me. I was wearing my favourite red salwar-kameez that Mum changed me into from the hospital gown. I was fortunate to die a married woman with sindhoor in the parting of my hair and bangles in my hands. I heard the 70-year-old neighbour share how she was living the life of a widow. My dad and husband were now standing to my left. Mum was at home with my son. Before leaving, she'd kissed my forehead.

I looked around and saw a handful of pyres burning; the families and friends looked just like those of mine. There was a sense of quiet, interrupted occasionally by the sounds of weeping, car horns, soft whispers, mantras, phones and footsteps.

There were many questions.

'How did it happen?'

'When did she breathe her last?'

The story of Monday's accident was repeated with finer details, every time. People sought answers, concern obvious in their eyes, especially about the future of my seven-year-old boy. The adults would soon come to terms with losing me; it's always tougher for the child. A 35-year-old colleague, who lost her mother when she was only 11, was saying so.

I began to think of my own mother's words to me as I had held my son in my arms for the first time, 'When you become a mother, you're never really alone in your thoughts.' She understood when I asked for help. 'Mum, can you watch over him while I take a quick shower?'

My husband walked around the pyre three times, something I'd heard the priest telling him he'd have to do. As he went along, he sprinkled a few drops of water on the pyre from a copper vessel the priest had handed over to him. I could read his mind. I'd known him for nine years. He was thinking of the times he'd sprinkled water on my eyes to wake me up on weekends. It was our little game. I'd be awake, but I'd wait for him to tease me and sprinkle the water, 'Wake up, lazybones.' Then we'd sit in the balcony and have our coffee as we listed the weekend's chores. I knew he was thinking about the last coffee we'd had. I could see him falling apart with each step. But he and I both knew that this time I wasn't pretending; the water drops wouldn't rouse me. I was worried about him. I love him and knew I should have given him courage to stop his hand from shivering as he sprinkled ghee on the pyre. But as a mother with little time in hand, I had things to attend to before it was too late. Like my mum always said: 'A mother has to do what a mother has to do.'

The priest would soon ask my husband to light the pyre, perhaps the last time he'd ever look at my face, with the red sindhoor in my hair and a turmeric *tilaka* on my forehead. He'd been strong, but I feared at this point he'd break down. I wondered about the last communication between us. Maybe he'd say he'd miss me at every point in his life; maybe he'd be angry with me for leaving him; maybe he'd say he'd never stop loving me. He looked at me and said nothing, just wanting to memorise my face in a way he could never forget. Once the flame meets the wood and reaches me, I'd be slowly consumed by fire and there'd be nothing left. The spirit stays around till the service is complete and needs help to depart peacefully. The priest told my husband he'd have to complete all the rituals to give me a proper farewell.

A match was lit and I realised it really was time to leave; one last glance at my loved ones, then I excused myself to speak to my son. I had a lot to share and tell him, because, Mum, you're right, a mother is never alone in her thoughts.

Beta,

I know that at this moment you're very scared. Our house is full of people, a few you know, but many new faces too. I know you've never seen Granny cry so much. I know she's the one you always ran to when I scolded you. Today, as she sits next to you holding your hand, can I ask you to keep holding hers? Can you do that for me? If you too feel like crying, cry. And, if someone comes and tells you that 'boys don't cry', ignore them.

I want to tell you that it's okay to cry. Crying isn't a sign of weakness. Only those who feel and care can cry—the indifferent never shed a tear. And I know all the men in my life are caring individuals: you, your father and Grandpa.

Can you see your dad and grandpa around? Don't worry if you can't spot them; they're making phone calls and attending to the people who want to say goodbye to me. And I'll tell you a secret. They're both as scared as you are. I saw them cry too. They're hurt and sad, just like you are. And when I look at them, I know you too will grow up to be a strong man. Look at the way you're growing, taller each day, and I know that because the school uniform I bought for you in the summer is already looking short on you (remind Dad to get you a new one. The card with the address of the shop is in my cupboard's first drawer). I want you to understand that no matter how tall and strong you grow, you must never be afraid to feel, share and express pain.

We all feel pain; it just looks different on all of us. I know you're in pain right now, but soon you'll know what'll bring you comfort. Maybe it'll be eating your favourite pancakes with Nutella, or hiding behind your fighter planes. Maybe you'll like sitting alone and doing your spellings or maybe you won't want to study at all. Maybe you'll feel like breaking your new car or just lying in bed. Don't be afraid. Find your comfort. And while you do that, let those around you find their own ways out of pain too, and respect how they choose to deal with it.

There's nothing wrong with being in pain and you have a right to grieve, but remember that you should never let losing me compromise your life or the lives of those around you. See if there's dirt in your nails; if it's been too long since you cut them, attend to that. If your grades start falling, pull up your socks and open your books. If you notice Dad's been quiet for too long, coax him into playing a game with you. If Granny or Grandpa looks weak, remind them to eat their meals and take their medicines on time. Once you've experienced and shared pain, use all your strength to show up at school, the dining table and birthday parties.

The pain you feel right now will never disappear completely, but I promise it'll slowly fade. The tears will cease and over time, you'll find new ways to remember me: photos of us on holidays, the cards you drew for me, the tantrums you threw, the sandwiches we made together and the nights I fell asleep, putting you to bed. Cherish what we had.

This isn't the first time you'll experience pain, though it'll probably hurt the longest. As you grow up, your heart will often be broken. I wish I could speak to you about how a girl might cheat on you or how a friend may betray you in college. A colleague might take credit for your work and an important order may slip from your hands. Maybe Granny and Grandpa will fall sick and you'll have to say goodbye to them. Sometimes, you'll feel like crying and throwing it all in. Don't. Never give up. Remember—to be a winner, you have to be at the starting line. Keep on showing up for job interviews, meetings and weddings. Life may hurt you many times, but never let the pain engulf you; if you do, you'll miss seeing the smiles that await you. Always show up after the storm: a fight, a death or a lost match.

I know last week you and I had a little discussion about how many candies you are allowed in a week, and it made you upset. I loved having these talks with you; arguments and discussions are part of growing up. But remember never to make the issues bigger than the people you argue with. I know you and Dad will argue about many things. Maybe you'll be upset over the curfew time he'd set for returning home after a party; maybe he'll disapprove of your hairstyle; maybe you won't like what he's cooked for you; maybe you'll be annoyed with him when he drives the car slowly. Just try to be patient. And most importantly, as Granny told me: 'Never leave home in anger or go straight to bed after an argument.'

Once when I was 10, I was very cross when my bike broke. I screamed at Grandpa when he wasn't able to fix it, flung myself on my bed and wept till I slept. When I woke up the next morning, Granny told me Grandpa had woken up early to fix my bike. I wanted to rush up to him and thank him with a warm hug, but he'd left for a work trip. I had to wait for three days to give him that hug.

It's not that arguments and fights are bad things, or that getting upset over them is wrong. I'm just saying that you should never make a disagreement so big that you can't overlook it. I want you to know that telling someone you love them despite any disputes you might have is important, and that you should never have to wait too long to tell someone that. Sometimes the wait can be forever, so never walk out in anger.

I understand that you're very upset with Dad. I know he told you I'd gone away for work and would be back by the weekend. I also know he tried to explain why I wouldn't be coming back, but both you and I know that Dad is bad at talking and explaining. So please listen, because I want you to understand what happened.

Remember on Tuesday, when you woke up, I wasn't at home and couldn't drop you off at school? At breakfast, Dad told you I was travelling for work for a few days. On Monday night, after putting you to sleep, I went to the market and met with a road accident. Dad rushed me to the hospital. And while Granny and Grandpa took care of you, he helped the doctors look after me. I was fast asleep, but the doctors told Daddy he'd be able to take me home by Sunday, so that's what he told you. They never thought I wouldn't be back. You know how much Mamma loves being with you. Remember when you started school and I joked I'd apply too, so I could be with you all the time? The doctors and Daddy tried everything, but they couldn't revive me, and I know this hurts them as much as it hurts you and me. They tried again today, but it didn't work.

I couldn't wake up and I'm very sorry about that. I died this morning and can't return. I want to say this to you because I want you to know that I never wanted to leave you alone, ever. I know you'll understand. You're a big boy. Sometimes, people have to die, like the heroes in your book. 'Mamma has now become a star in the sky and she'll always watch over you.' I know Dad told you that. Believe him.

I'm sad about leaving you, but you must know I lived a beautiful life and I want you to live a beautiful one too. I want you to enjoy each day to the fullest, just as I did. Never be in such a hurry that you don't notice a crescent moon or a ladybird on a flower. Watch cartoons and enjoy spreading peanut butter on the toast. When you grow up and pick a sport (I think it'll be cricket; you never go anywhere without your bat and ball), remember to enjoy each moment on the field. Always open doors for the elderly and never be so preoccupied that you miss helping out the needy. Take pleasure in little moments. Remember to live and not to race. And when you leave home for further studies and later a job, always wish Dad happy birthday, and remind Grandpa and Granny to go for their medical check-ups. These things might seem insignificant compared to the prizes you'll win at school or the promotions you'll earn at work, but just like that tiny puzzle piece you needed to finish your *Lion King* picture, these little things are important to make your life complete. Family albums, friends' weddings and office farewells matter just as much as CVs, portfolios and awards. Maybe a backyard picnic will seem insignificant when you have tickets for a tour of Europe in your bag, but still have that picnic.

And as you go along, always remember to make good friends. You know what they say about friends. They're people we pick for ourselves, for the fun stuff. I found a good few and shared wonderful times with them. There's no greater happiness in life than having friends you can call family. I hope you build a lovely family of friends.

Also, don't worry too much about how many friends you make. Add up the number of years you've known the ones you have. Nurture your friendships.

I know I've mentioned you'll find a good job, but before that you have to attend school, college and university. I know you'll do well; you're such a bright boy. Remember, education is very important, don't leave it midway. You mightn't like all the subjects or score well across the board, but I'm sure you'll soon find which subject you enjoy studying the most. Never be afraid to try something new or follow your dreams. Don't be scared to fail and fall. Maybe your interests will change every month, every year. Don't worry about that, it happens to all of us.

It's always tough selecting a profession, so choose wisely and commit to work that you'll look forward to doing each day. Your career should be one of the most important reasons you wake up in the morning. Choose what you like doing, then stick at it. Don't let excuses like lack of time, personal commitments and bruised egos keep you away from work.

Build a life outside home and take pride in it. I never missed a day at work, but I never brought my work home, either. Try to keep that balance.

And yes, I really wish you fall in love, like Mamma and Papa did. I know you'll grow up to be a handsome boy just like your dad, and I'll miss standing next to you as you marry the woman you love. I'll also miss teasing you when dates go wrong and worrying about what you get up to behind my back.

When you're married, don't let your dad down, but most importantly, don't let yourself down. Marriage is hard and there'll be fights, egos, adjustments and compromises. Celebrate good days *and* bad days. Drink to the collapses, cheers, failures, successes, mistakes and learnings. Somewhere in between, you'll fall in love with each other, all over again.

Speak to your dad on difficult days, invite him over for football matches (I'm sure he'll love that) and talk man to man. If he says the opposite of what you want to hear, just hear him out. He's very wise. But if you choose not to follow his advice, that's fine too. Remember each life story is different and no one knows yours better than you. Work towards your 'happy ever after'.

But there's one advice Dad will give you that I do want you to follow. Love your wife for her strengths *and* her weaknesses. Argue with her, but hear her out too. Take care of her and let her take care of you. It's not too bad if you occasionally forget to open the car door for her, but it is important to let her know you respect her as an individual. And when you become parents, love each other a little more.

I don't know how much longer I can go on. But I trust you can take care of your father; he probably won't tell you, but there'll be days when he'll want to give up too. Tickle his feet: it'll make him smile. And when he grows old, be patient with him. If he doesn't answer the phone, don't be upset—he may have been asleep, or can't operate the fancy phone you bought him fast enough. If he doesn't answer after a second call, he may need your help. Visit him or ask the neighbours to check on him.

Do the same for your grandparents. Try to spend time with both of them. They'll look for me in you; let them feel the warmth.

And as your father grows old and you cut more birthday cakes, encourage each other to stay healthy. Take out time for running or swimming, join a gym or play sport. Eat healthily; remember you mightn't be able to show up for work or parties if you're in poor health. Eat the wafers and burgers, but not too many. I am confident that you will find a way to learn that anything in excess is bad. I am also sure you'll find a way to stay away from sin, evil and harm. I know as a young boy, you might be tempted to smoke, hurl abuse and flirt with women, but I know, you will have the wisdom to know when to stop.

I know I have spoken of things that are difficult for you to understand right now. But I wish one day you find courage, wisdom and love in these words. I'm hoping these words will serve as a checklist, one that you'd like to keep coming back to as you grow up. At various stages in life, new challenges will be thrown your way and I wish you emerge victorious, each time.

Don't worry if you forget to follow all of what I'm saying, but remember one thing—be happy. I found my definition of happiness in my work and family, our meals and conversations, the holidays we took and the movies we watched. I surrounded myself with things that made my heart smile and made me feel beautiful. Don't worry about leading a good or bad life. No one can judge how well you've lived, but having a life filled with happy moments is down to you. Work towards that.

I'm worried it's time for me to go and I've still not spoken about family values and traditions. I can only hope that you'll have absorbed these lessons from being with me and your dad. I wanted to speak to you about the importance of saving enough for a rainy day. I am sure Dad will teach you that. I wanted to tell you never to cheat, and if someone does it to you, breathe in before you react. Don't tolerate cruelty or dishonesty, but never take it upon yourself to punish wrong-doers—remember, it isn't your job. I wanted to tell you how to clean your wounds with antiseptic. And what's best for breakfast. But I'm afraid I have to go now.

I know you're scared and want me to stay a little longer. But I can't. Don't panic. Dad and Grandpa too will be here soon; they're making preparations to send me off and I know you'd want that done properly. So don't be upset. I know Dad is looking out for you. He just told your aunt that you were excited about next week's fancy dress competition. Don't worry. She'll help you dress up and I know you'll make the perfect pirate. Just show up if you can. But if you want to cuddle and sleep in your dad's arms, just do that.

And remember, I'll never stop loving you.

Love,

Mamma

*****

ACKNOWLEDGEMENTS

The Trees Told Me So is both a milestone and a beginning.

At this moment, I am grateful for the collapses and cheers as well as excited to strive harder and dream bigger.

First, thanks to Vishal, my husband. While writing a book is tough, living with an author-to-be is far more challenging. His vocabulary for a job well done is limited to 'nice', but I'm glad that he kept repeating the word with varied prefixes, each time I reached out to him for feedback. He is now equipped to write his own book titled *How to live with (and love) a moody writer.* We made it till here, together. *Nice.*

Mummy-Papa, I can never thank you enough for encouraging me to write. During my growing-up years, I kept a diary in which I documented all my experiences. Also, I scribbled songs and poems on little notepads that came free with candy boxes. On many occasions, I wrote letters to my parents as they sat in the other room. They never threw a single piece of paper or diary away or told me I was being silly.

We all need a sounding board, mine is Prachi, my sister. I can't recall a single phone call between us when I didn't express my wish to write a book and later discussed the paraphernalia. I also can't recall a single instance when she complained or expressed boredom when I repeated myself. Until date, I haven't taken any decision without running it through her and I'll not have it any other way. She still attends my calls. I will call her and thank her when I'm done writing this note.

It's scary to share your words for the first time with anyone and a few people made it easier for me. Geetika Nautiyal, my friend of 15 years, who took out the time to read each single email with the subject line, 'Read Pls'. Her reply always began with, 'Puru, I am so happy to read this'. Fiona Cochrane, my first virtual NaNoWriMo partner. Was it not for her, I would not have been able to push myself to write more or stop editing.

Fiona Paterson, who critiqued each story with kindness and patience. Kanika Kalra, for her email titled, 'To, Author PG'. Anne Cherian, for being the 2am friend. Sonu Sultania, for promising to wait for a signed copy. Ravi Sabnani, for treating me like a published author from the day we met. Sangeetha Bhaskaran, for reminding me that craziness is a brilliant trait. Thank you.

A shout out to Suhail Mathur, my literary agent. The Book Bakers, who finds it endearing that I call him S. S.; it was a pleasure to work with you.

Finally, thank you, Niyogi Publishers, for your faith in my words, and Manali Das, for the wonderful edits.

*****

GLOSSARY

Avatar: incarnation

Bale: a Mehendi design where a row of flowers and stems run from the ring finger to the wrist, front and back—like a wreath

Bali: Earring

Chatai: a plastic woven floor mat

Cheeni: sugar crystals

Choolah: stove

Chuna: limestone powder and water

Elaichi: cardamom

Gulab: rose petals

Gulkand:	rose preserve
Heera panna:	a mix of vegetable and fruit powder
Jeera:	cumin
Jhuggi:	a slum house made of mud
Jutti:	a footwear common in North India, mostly made of leather and decorated with colourful embroidery
Kattha:	a paste of catechu and water
Kesari supari:	grated saffron betel nut
Khajoor:	dates
Langar:	a free communal meal
Laung:	clove
Malai:	cream
Manjaa:	a traditional woven bed
Mitti:	dirt
Mundan:	the act of shaving off babies' birth hair, believed to carry undesirable traits from past lives, is another age-old Hindu custom
Namak:	salt
Namkeen:	a salty mixture of corn flakes, peanuts and spices
Pardes:	abroad
Pasina:	sweat

Pucca ghar:	a house with a solid roof
Pudina:	mint
Saada:	plain
Saunf:	fennel seeds
Shahad:	honey
Sookha nariyal:	dry coconut powder
Supari:	diced betel nut
Tehravin:	a traditional Hindu ceremony conducted to mark the final day of mourning on the 13th day after one's death
Tilaka:	a vermillion mark on the forehead
Zardosi:	beautiful metal embroidery work

*****